SYSTEMA PARADOXA

ACCOUNTS OF CRYPTOZOOLOGICAL IMPORT

VOLUME 17

SAND AND SECRETS

A TALE OF THE MONGOLIAN DEATH WORM

AS ACCOUNTED BY ROBERT GREENBERGER

NEOPARADOXA

Pennsville, NJ

2023

PUBLISHED BY
NeoParadoxa
A division of eSpec Books
PO Box 242
Pennsville, NJ 08070
www.especbooks.com

ISBN: 978-1-949691-93-1
ISBN (ebook): 978-1-949691-92-4

Interior Design: Danielle McPhail
www.sidhenadaire.com

Cover Art: Jason Whitley
Cover Design: Mike and Danielle McPhail, McP Digital Graphics
Interior Illustration: Jason Whitley

Copyediting: Greg Schauer and John L. French

DEDICATION

FOR JEFF ROVIN,
WHO INVITED ME INTO THE REALM OF THE WEIRD,
GAVE ME ROOM TO EXPLORE, AND OFFERED ME
POSSIBLY THE BEST DAY JOB I'VE EVER HELD.

CHAPTER ONE

"Devushka, may I make your acquaintance?"

The words, delivered in heavily accented English, startled Ella Trigiani, absorbed as she was with the video on her laptop screen. There, a pair of Amur Leopards raced and played in the night air, preparatory to mating. Whoever shot the video had used powerful equipment, set on a tripod, and was able to zoom in so she could see the sinewy muscles ripple beneath their sleek fur. They were beautiful and she had been daydreaming a bit about being in the field to see them for herself.

As a result, she didn't hear the older student enter the conference room or even sense his presence. She turned to look at him. He was tall, pale, his light brown hair in a Caesar cut — something she thought was long out of style — and clad in an open yellow dress shirt and tight jeans. He was probably a grad student, also researching at the Zoological Museum of Moscow University, but she hadn't seen him before. His angular face was handsome enough, although he needed a shave. The dark beard looked out of place, giving him a sinister countenance. He was definitely checking her out with open interest, which made her feel somewhat uncomfortable.

"Good morning," she said in passable Russian. It had taken her a solid year to master enough of the language to be ready for the three-month stint in Russia, but she had few troubles with being understood. She had hoped she had all the right words to indicate her disinterest; she wasn't in Russia for a boyfriend but for her studies.

"Good morning to *you*," he repeated. "I am Rodion Belyaev." He said this with some pride, and she half-expected he waited for her to recognize the name. She let it pass.

"Ella Trigiani," she announced and thrust out a hand for a shake. He took it, his warm skin not unpleasant, as he squeezed lightly and pumped once.

"Italian, no?"

"Italian-American, yes," she said.

"Da. So, what brings you to this dreary conference room?" he asked, remaining close.

"I am here for three months, studying Russian animal life before I begin graduate school."

"Here, I hope?"

She had to force herself not to roll her eyes when she replied, "No, sorry, I'll be studying at Bucknell."

"Where is this?"

"Pennsylvania, in the east," she said. It was a source of pride that she got into the challenging program the same week she landed this paid internship.

"Never heard of it," he said dismissively. "You should be here, in Moscow, to master the language and the animals." *And you can master me, no doubt,* she thought.

"These," he said, gesturing to the leopards on the screen, "they spend much time in the trees. Do you like to climb?"

"Not really. I'm more of a hiker."

"Ah. Well, what you're looking at, they're rare," he said, now leaning over her shoulder for a better look, the morning coffee still on his breath. She found his closeness bothersome but withstood it.

As the two continued to talk, she slowly found him engaging and agreed to meet for lunch later. Not that she was interested, but since her arrival a week earlier, she'd been viewed as an exhibit as opposed to a colleague. The tensions between their countries led to suspicions but hse had hoped academia was protected from political enmity. No such luck it seemed. She'd been stared at, nodded to, and ignored, but few actually bothered to speak to her, beyond the mentor she had been assigned, and he was more distracted than helpful. If nothing else, Rodion would help sharpen her conversational Russian, an asset for her internship.

One meal stretched to two, then drinks after work. Within days, she realized he intrigued her, sharing like interests despite entirely different worldviews. They both liked some of the same drama films and pop music of the previous decade. They differed, naturally, when it came to politics, so early on they silently agreed to steer clear. In some ways, Rodion seemed like a throwback, a man from an earlier era—the proud, boastful Russian—and he delighted in the role. Not that she had dated much during college, just the occasional hookups and one serious boyfriend, but none of them had held doors or pulled out her chair. At restaurants and bars, he ensured she had plenty of water and insisted on pouring the wine. And he always paid, actually insisting on it. Once in the ladies' room, an older woman who had seen them together, explained the "macho" Russian male was not a myth and Rodion well exemplified the behavior. She suspected he couldn't always afford it on a grad student's pay, but their only real arguments were over this point. Ella had money from her stipend, so was willing to buy the occasional meal or round of drinks, but he wouldn't hear of it, tossing his credit card like a frisbee, signing the receipt without a glance.

"Imagine, a 24,000-year-old worm is found in the permafrost, and we revive it, and it decides to reproduce as if it was just another day," he marveled one night.

Global climate change was a disaster for the world at large, but for scientists, the softening land yielded up its secrets. The rotifer had been found in Siberian permafrost giving rise to a new train of thought regarding suspended animation.

"Once they're done with that, they will no doubt work their way up the food chain. Maybe we are studying the wrong thing."

"No, I like my mammals, thank you," she said.

To make his case about her needing to be more open-minded, he took her to a screening of *Zoology*, the Ivan I. Tverdovsky movie about the lonely zookeeper who miraculously grew a tail. "See, stick with those warm-blooded beasts, and you too will have a tail."

He made her laugh. And think. She was willing to deal with his antiquated manners since he more than made up for it with conversation.

"You should stay here, get your doctorate," Rodion told her on their third date. In America, the third date usually suggested sex, but he didn't push the matter, instead pouring on the charm. She'd now been warned about Russian men from other women and while he fit the stereotype, he also had a keen, inquisitive mind in a field she appreciated. That gave them a connection that might withstand his blunt ways.

"You'd be a few years behind me, but ah, what adventures we would have."

"My visa is only for the three-month program," Ella protested. He made a dismissive sound as if the red tape wasn't a barrier. "Besides, I really had my heart set on working in San Diego. The zoo there is incredible."

"So I hear," he said, although the noncommittal tone improbably suggested he'd heard of San Diego, maybe not their zoo.

"Look, Rodion, I am all set to get my MS in Zoology at Bucknell. I haven't even started thinking about a doctorate. By then, I'll probably just want to get started."

"So, no office job for you? Out in the field instead?"

"I picked mammals because I can get close, see them, and interact. Often there's an intelligence there that I find fascinating," she explained.

"You want a conversation with a lion?"

She chuckled but shook her head. Her loose, curly brown hair waved around her. "I want to work with them, to protect them." To her mind, she sounded overly earnest, but she truly loved them and wanted to help protect them as their environment shrank and climate change threatened them and way too many species. She had no idea how she could to protect them, but it wasn't necessarily going to be from a lab and most certainly not from a classroom.

"No, but I do want to get out there, study them in the wild, and then figure out how to help them," she said.

"So, you are an idealist," he said with a laugh.

"Not at all. But you, why do you want to be a zoologist?"

"Ah, well, we share the world with them, and as it gets hotter and more dangerous, they need someone to understand them, watch out for them," he said.

"So, you want to understand a lion," she said, mocking his voice.

He threw back his head and laughed loudly at that, causing others to turn and look their way. Ella blushed a bit at this but enjoyed the banter. At first, she had worried that all this charm meant he expected her to sleep with him before getting to know him. But it became clear as he escorted her home each night, he didn't expect an invitation in. When she asked him about it, he shrugged, something he did often, and said, "It's what a man does. He escorts his woman home, makes sure she is safe." *His* woman caught her off-guard, but she let it slide.

He was getting intimate, in his own way; his hand at the small of her back, guiding her through a restaurant. There were gentle touches of her shoulders or arms, fingers brushing against her own, as he helped her on or off with her coat, something she was surprised she still needed as summer approached. Within days, he started caressing her mane of long, brown hair, something that was definitely out of style among Russian women, who were gorgeous, dressed to the nines, and always perfectly presented to the public. As he deposited her at her door, he'd kiss her fore-head, a gesture he also began doing any time he left them, even for a moment. He'd begun enveloping her smaller frame in his arms, warming her heart but also signaling to every other male in sight that Ella was off-limits. Talk about studying animal behavior…

Ella was charmed by the little gifts he brought her, or she found at her workstation. She had amassed quite the collection of gaudy gold animals, which now circled her laptop, protecting it. He'd show up with flowers now and then so the small flat she had been assigned was fragrant.

This was why, two weeks in, when he brought her to the door at the end of another wonderful meal, he reached down to kiss her forehead and she reached up to kiss his lips. It had been long enough, she decided. The building tension had reached a fever pitch. She found him smart, funny, attractive, and in his own semi-neanderthal way, charming. He responded with fervor, and the kiss lingered, but that's where she ended it. Anything else could wait and she was sure he *would* wait, and she suspected he'd be worth it. They had bonded, there was now a mutual un-spoken obligation to one another, that would reach its conclusion in time. She found she wasn't in a rush to consummate matters, as long as they continued in this manner.

On the night she expected it to happen — at last — he surprised her with a text message asking her to meet him in the museum after hours. During the day, the high-ceilinged, well-lit museum boasted halls with dark green arches and orange-and-white tiled floors, with murals between each arch. Some rooms had paintings and drawings high up the walls, while glass cases boasted a wide variety of exhibits. It was a crown jewel in the museum system, the second largest zoology museum in the large country.

They were to meet at seven after the public was shooed out, but before the entire complex went dark for the night, guards and custodians kept the exhibits company until dawn. Ella found him by his own workspace, a messy affair with papers, journals, and catalogs, burying his laptop. A small statue of a brown bear was the only decoration that might be considered personal. A mug still half-full of cold coffee bore the museum logo, suggesting he treated this as only a transitory location, not worth leaving his mark.

"Good," Rodion said by way of greeting as he entered. He had on a purple shirt and jeans, his rainbow assortment of button-downs the only change to his routine. He wore the same scuffed black boots every day, seemed to own one or a dozen pairs of the same worn jeans, and he must see the barber with regularity because the hair never seemed to change. He did, though, shave daily, something she had nudged him into doing, his one great concession for her approval.

"Why are we here?" Ella asked.

"I have planned a great adventure for us, and it starts tonight with a *draznit*,"

She blinked, unable to understand the final word. "I'm sorry, what?"

"Draznit… uh, a taste, a tease," he stammered out, a rare kink in his impervious armor. He opened a misaligned desk drawer, pulling hard on it. It opened with a protesting groan and he reached in for a keyring. More than a dozen keys of varying sizes and shapes dangled from the large steel ring, and he playfully tossed them in the air, catching them as his hip shoved the drawer closed.

"Come, *moya lyubov*, let me share a secret with you."

Curious, Ella followed him into portions of the museum she hadn't been in before. They were narrow utility halls leading toward the very back of the building. Only low-emergency lights were on, and a musty smell mixed with cleaning fluids hung in the air. Cartons and spare furniture turned the path into an obstacle course, but she never was more than two strides behind him. He walked with practiced confidence, the keys bobbing in his right hand as he whistled some tune she didn't know. Finally, they reached a door on the right-hand side, and he tossed the keyring high in the air, snatching it with emphasis, and then quickly flipped through the options, settling on one that didn't seem all that special. It slid noiselessly into the lock, and he opened the door, which was also quiet. Beyond it was a staircase leading only down.

Ella followed him, straining against the gloom to try and see if there was any signage, any clue as to where they were or where they were headed. The blank walls mocked her inquiry. They descended two flights into a subbasement she didn't know existed. The stairs led them right into a cinderblock space which flared to life as he flipped a series of switches, activating the overhead banks of fluorescent lighting. The room was large, twenty by thirty feet. A worn, wooden desk was jammed against one wall but most of the other space was filled with traditional filing cabinets, flat files stacked three sets high, and other storage units. Nothing was on display, although there were two tables in the center, with magnifying apparatus and ring lighting.

He let her absorb it, a grin on his face.

"What is this?"

"This grand museum we work in was built on a man's love for invertebrates but we, we defiant young pups prefer our mammals, eh? Johann Fischer von Waldheim brought his catalog when he was our director. Until we opened to the public in 1866, just after your most uncivil war, everything was kept private."

Rodion continued to play with the keyring as he walked over to the flat files. He studied some coding and opened a drawer about a third of the way down, gesturing for her to join him. When she peered over his shoulder, she discovered the decayed remains of a bat, sandwiched between layers of glass.

"But, not everything was shown to the public. No, the museum, like so much of my country, loves its secrets. Some of our finds were considered ordinary or too poisonous. Some considered certain breeds so hideous that the directors feared women would faint or children would scream."

Both chuckled at the provincial thinking from nearly two centuries previous.

"But, moya lyubov, some were kept hidden because no one knew what they were."

"Unknown species?"

"Da. Tell me, does your homeland have gorodskiye legendy... urban legends?"

Ella laughed at that as she ransacked her memory for tales her grandmother told her growing up. She was an immigrant, raised in Italy, and relocated after World War II.

"Don't we all? Yes, I recall my nonna telling me scary stories at Halloween. She told me about Thryus, a dragon, and Striga, some sort of demon. So yes, we have our legends."

"Good, good. Our world is definitely filled with legends and unknown species, like that ancient rotifer. Some have been found and kept hidden because we don't fully understand them. We are going to help change that." His confidence bordered on bravado, but Ella had no clue what he was going on about.

With a flourish, he flipped the keys into the air once more, then, as they settled, he found a small one that fit into a black cabinet in the corner. He slowly opened the double doors and then slipped on thin, white protective gloves before withdrawing something framed. He brought it to the examination table with some ceremony and laid it down for her scrutiny.

Ella walked over to peer through the old, dim glass. Pressed between two panes were what she first thought to be the shed skin of a reptile. But then she saw it was thicker than a normal snake and segmented. Small protrusions of some sort ringed each segment. It had a reddish cast to it but was faded. What then caught her eye was the head, which seemed to have two sharp pincers. No, maybe there were more, but decayed.

"What is this?"

"That, dear Ella, is a legend, the Olgoï-Khorkhoï… Mongolian Death Worm."

"The *what*? I never heard of a death worm."

"Of course not," he laughed. "It is a legend; it does not exist."

"Then what I am looking at?"

"That, dushka, is the question."

She continued to stare at the desiccated remains, but she also began to feel tension fill her body. Something told her to be wary of this dead thing. She stifled a shudder, biting her lip and feeling foolish for doing that. This was a reptile of some sort, misidentified by someone hoping to have discovered something new.

"It is said to exist and one of your countrymen was the first to write about it. There have been sightings, stories told from nomad to nomad, and a legend has grown. But, my darling, no one has managed to capture one."

"But this…"

"This, Ella, is a portion of a dead worm that was recovered and secreted here for study in 1972. You will not find it in the databases, nor will you find anything about it upstairs."

"I don't understand. Why are you showing it to me?"

"Well, first, I like showing you things," he said with a broad smile. She'd come to love that smile. "Second, you are an intern, here to learn. This is something they will never teach you at your Bucknell."

"Because it doesn't exist?"

"Da! But, most importantly, I wanted you to see this because this is the first step on our adventure, the one I promised you."

"A worm, if that's what it is, doesn't fit into my mammalian studies," she protested.

"Da, da, it does not. But you want to be a zoologist. You told me you want to be in the field. I am taking you into the field!"

"Where? What are you talking about?"

"Ella, moya lyubov, I have arranged for us to join an expedition in search of the Mongolian Death Worm!"

Ella felt her jaw drop in surprise before she could control herself. There was something she disliked about the remains and the notion of seeing one in person was disquieting. More than that, he was proposing they go in search of a legend.

"You do know this sounds crazy," she said.

"Da, but it is not crazy, but a reality. Allow me to elaborate. My mentor, Professor Lehya Kuznetsov, has been pursuing funding to find a living example of this since his mentor first showed him this very specimen decades ago. I don't know how he did it, but he finally secured the money and has been preparing for this trip. Three days ago, I convinced him to invite me to be a part of it, and it has taken me that long to convince him to bring you along."

"Why me?"

"You're here to learn, so if we find this, then you will be learning something no one else of your generation has even conceived of. I know, I know, it is invertebrate, but who cares? This will be the find of the century, and you want your name associated with this. And, let's be real here, a Russian's word is not so good overseas. An American witness will give us... doveriye."

"Credence? That it will," she said. And should something go wrong, she realized with a slight shudder, an American was more expendable than one of their own countrymen.

"But seriously, do you even think you can find this worm?"

"Kuznetsov does, and I believe him."

"Where is the expedition going?"

"The Gobi Desert. The creature is only seen there and then only during the wet season, so we go in July."

"This is crazy, Rodion," she said. Her mind was excited about actually going on an expedition. Even if they found nothing, it would give her immense experience. It meant more time with this man and that she found both very appealing and very confounding. Still, warning bells sounded in the recesses of her mind, suggesting that there was definitely a danger beyond the most inhospitable biome he wanted to take her. It certainly gave new meaning to the term hot date.

"No, this is destiny calling. Will you answer it?"

"That is so corny," she said.

"Corny?"

She thought a moment, then suggested, "Banal,no?"

Rodion nodded in understanding, smiling at the word. "Not romantichnyy?"

Ella shook her head at that. "The Gobi Desert is not at all the definition of romantichnyy nor is the idea of looking for a worm." She inwardly shuddered at that thought.

"Well, no matter. It is all arranged."

"It is? What about my own work?"

"Your supervisor will be supportive," he said matter-of-factly.

Which reminded her of the worst aspect of getting involved with Rodion, or any other Russian. He had little respect, well none to be precise, for her schedule and needs. It didn't matter if she had a hair appointment or had made plans with a coworker. He just presumed she'd rearrange her life to make herself available. Apparently, this was ingrained in all Russian men, something the one female coworker she'd befriended, Yelena, confirmed just the day before.

"What if I don't want to go worm hunting?"

Rodion stared at her in disbelief, as if she spoke in Klingon, not Russian. He acted as if her coming was a done deal. But was it? She had to decide what she was going to do. His domineering approach made her want to reject the prospect just on principle. But despite her hivemind warnings, the idea of an expedition, a hunt intrigued her. The experience would be invaluable toward her grad program, giving her a leg up over the others. But would the opportunity be worth rearranging her whole itinerary? Of course, there was also the matter of Rodion, who was, ahem, 'worming' his way into her heart. She didn't like the idea of time away from each other just as things seemed about to go to the next level. They had nowhere near enough time as it was, so slicing a chunk out wouldn't help.

She stared at the remains a bit longer, mulling over the pros and cons, when Rodion abruptly drew them away and returned them to the cabinet. He locked up and gestured for them to leave. She dutifully exited the lab, her brain and heart having a debate she only partially paid attention to. They quietly left the building and went to the pub for drinks. Not once did he bring up the expedition, discussing other issues and topics. To him, the matter was decided, and there was nothing left to discuss. For Ella, there was plenty to discuss but seemingly little point, a growing source of frustration for her. Rodion acted as if all had been decided, with all the administrative details addressed before her opinion was even solicited. That her wishes were not considered relevant to not sit well with her, another reason staying in Russia held little appeal.

Somewhere after their third beer, her body seemed to reach a consensus. She was done thinking for now. It was time to act. When Rodion escorted her to her flat and kissed her chastely, she held on as she unlocked the door and dragged him in.

CHAPTER TWO

The next week was crazy.

Despite Rodion's promises, his supervisor wasn't really interested in adding an American mammalian grad student to his team. She wasn't all that surprised and accepted the fact that just as they had grown closer, they would be separated. By the time he returned, she'd be heading home. He fumed and furiously proclaimed he'd fix it, but nothing seemed to change.

A shadow crossed her workspace, the silhouette not the one she had come to recognize and expect. Ella looked up and saw the woman from the restroom weeks earlier. She was in her forties, with a severe look, her hair tight behind her head. Everything about her said no nonsense.

"Are you truly interested in Lehya Kuznetsov's expedition?" she asked without greeting.

Ella checked herself. Instinctively, she wanted to say no, but she had to consider the value of genuine field experience. The worm was probably nothing special, but the chance to be out there, seeing the wildlife for herself, was incredibly tempting. She nodded.

"Is it for the boy?"

Without hesitation, she shook her head.

"You are studying mammals, yes? The reports say you are a good researcher. So, why?"

"Wherever Professor Kuznetsov goes, there are likely to be mammals, and I would love to see them for myself. It would be a unique experience for field work."

"Da. But it also presents dangers. You are an American which presents other complications. For me to get permission for you to join them, and all the paperwork that would follow, I need your assurance this for science, not sex."

Ella appreciated her bluntness and nodded before saying, "I would go even if Rodion remained behind. This is for my future and my career."

The woman nodded in confirmation, then turned and walked away without a word, leaving Ella somewhat stunned. Who was she?

As it turned out, she was Valeriya Lomonosov, a director of the program. Another three days passed with Rodion fuming and Ella ignoring her growing desire to be in the desert. Then came the morning her inbox contained an email with a dozen different files attached, all of them legal waivers to permit her to leave Russia for the Gobi Desert, limited liability for the Russian program, and other documents. An hour later came a terse note from Kuznetsov's assistant, with details on the trip.

She was going to the Gobi Desert!

Ella worked late to complete her current assignment, but her supervisor's heavy-lidded eyes gave her pause. With a grunt, he assented, but his body language and extra tasks indicated he wasn't entirely on board with the plan. Still, she was cleared to go.

In between completing her required tasks, Ella devoted herself to doing research on the Gobi and what would be required. Professor Kuznetsov proved a welcoming figure, providing her with packing checklists and pointed her to recommended websites to learn about the Gobi.

What wasn't discussed was the Mongolian Death Worm itself. After all, the museum didn't admit to the *subbasement* existing, let alone the remains of one specimen. In fact, their expedition was described as one in keeping with her specialty, seeking information on the Onager and the polecats, European and Marbled. She turned to the Internet and its web of trusted and untrustworthy websites. Ella was initially impressed at the number of websites and resources devoted to the mythical creature. Most seemed to agree on the basics: Mongolians had talked about this creature for some time before Roy Chapman Andrews first wrote about it in his 1926 work *On the Trail of Ancient Man*. There, Andrews quoted Mongolia's Prime Minister , who described it thusly: "It is shaped like a sausage about two feet long, has no head nor leg and it is so poisonous that merely to touch it means instant death. It lives in the most desolate parts of the Gobi Desert."

Despite Andrews repeating this information six years later in his follow-up book *The New Conquest of Central Asia*, he did not seem to believe in the creature's existence. That did not dissuade others from reporting on it and trying to locate it. She was amused to see several attempted expeditions try and fail to find it but refuse to doubt the worm existed. She did note that the creature had gained enough notoriety to be cited as the inspiration for Frank Herbert's mammoth sandworms in his seminal work *Dune*, something she kept meaning to read.

From other zoologists who actually understood the Gobi Desert, it was clear that the word worm was a misnomer as the creature had to be more like a snake or legless lizard, making it vertebrate. In theory, that meant bones would be found to confirm its existence; yet none have been identified.

Apparently, it survived underground except for the rainy period of June and July, emerging to lay eggs in whatever its prey was. It was said to spit an especially corrosive acid venom that reached several feet, leaving remains coated in yellow residue. Accounts of the Worm's actual size, shape, and appearance differed greatly, and a Google Image search showed all the variations, working from oral histories and no actual remains. She wondered what an artist would come up with using the remains locked away a few floors beneath her.

People seemed desperate to believe. When the venerable *Weekly World News* reported in 2009 about a giant sea worm captured in British waters, many claimed it to be a lost death worm or a relative. She also opted not to waste precious time on the self-titled SyFy feature film.

During this intense period, Rodion called with frightening regularity, checking on her. Was Ella getting cold feet? Had she started packing? Telling her she had enough coffee for the day, which is where she put her foot down. No one controlled her caffeine intake but her.

She worked late every day, even coming in on the weekend, to ensure everything got done so she could leave with a clean conscience. After work one Saturday, she went shopping for the desert, buying a proper rucksack, canteens, first aid supplies, and special clothing. Her stipend was stretched a bit, but once she and Rodion began spending time together, she hadn't had to pay for meals or drinks.

Despite her exhaustion, every evening ended with Rodion, who seemed totally unflappable. They'd eat something, drink a few beers, and then have some of the most amazing sex she had ever imagined. Still, she was concerned with his definition of their relationship. He seemed fully committed to her, fully invested, even as they continued to learn about one another. Ella was not so surprised that when she tried to describe herself as Rodion's girl-friend, there was no word for it, beyond girl and friend. This explained why he kept describing her as "his girl" and even once or twice called her, in front of coworkers, his bride. That startled her until it became clear from Yelena that this was how men thought and she was either going to accept it or break things off. By that point, she realized she had become as invested in the expedition as she was in Rodion so that wasn't really an option.

It wasn't until the night before they were to leave, that the full team assembled for a briefing followed by drinks. There would be three scientists leading the small party: Nicolai Smirnov, Sergei Lebedev, and Aleksandr Kozlov. Rodion and Ella were there to do the scut work and be the recorders for posterity. The Kremlin, which had to approve the trip, insisted on sending five soldiers, and thankfully, for Ella, one of them was female, so she would not be the sole woman. The soldiers were dismissive throughout Professor Kuznetsov's presentation, angering him. He was clearly too old to accompany them, entrusting the mission to others, but he made it clear he was in charge.

"You have to understand, we may never find it, but we need to find evidence, which we can only hope will bring us to its lair," the professor explained. "We need samples of the acid, of what it does to its victims, whatever we can ascertain."

"What do you propose we put it in should we capture this big worm?" the soldiers' leader, Timor Yegorov, asked. He was in his forties, a battle-hardened veteran, and took the assignment seriously even after vocally saying he thought the entire mission was a "bullshit waste of time."

"We will be bringing along several collapsible containers easily able to hold a five-foot worm," Kozlov said.

"What about the acid?" Yegorov challenged.

"You will be carrying bags of citric acid and sodium bicarbonate baking soda, which should neutralize its emissions," Kozlov said with confidence, but Ella had her concerns. A creature that large would emit more than just a small squirt.

"And the alcohol we're bringing is to treat acid burns, not for partying," Smirnov warned.

The soldiers groaned at that, although the woman added, "We'll bring our own!"

"You need to take this seriously," Kuznetsov snapped. "I have waited years for this to become a reality and you will not spoil it with childish behavior. If you find the creature, you must be very, very careful, and if the stars favor you, then you will bring back something that will help revolutionize science."

After the rotifer find, along with similar ancients being found, there seemed to be a new race going on among the science community and clearly these men were competitors.

Ella was uncertain about that pronouncement. Yes, finding the mythical creature would would add to man's understanding of the world. But revolutionize science? That sounded rather grandiose.

They reviewed the flight path, where the camp would be established, and a quick check of the day-by-day itinerary.

Apparently, they'd set up a base camp and go off in different directions based on evidence found in the Gobi. It was a little vague for Ella's taste, but as the most junior member of the team, she kept that to herself. Kuznetsov expected daily updates by satellite phone along with downloads of the data recorded by his trusted interns. There was definitely fatherly pride shown to Rodion, who beamed in the approbation. Ella was glad for him since it showed he had earned his way on.

Given the early flight the following day, she agreed to let Rodion and his gear spend the night — a first. They would celebrate the trip with abandon since they would need to be far more circumspect once they were in the desert.

When he fell asleep, she stared at the cracked, water-stained ceiling and couldn't decide if she was excited or scared or both. Her Bucknell advisor was thrilled for her, Ella's parents were far less enthusiastic. They didn't like her being in Russia, to begin with, and now the Gobi Desert, where they could only communicate by email, whenever circumstances allowed. But she was twenty-three now and making her own choices. This was her decision, and she was not going to back out, even as her hind mind reawakened the alarm bells.

CHAPTER THREE

Moscow was a gleaming metropolis. Its mix of traditional and modern architecture was captivating, and Ella enjoyed sightseeing as time permitted. She was far less enthralled with the bleak, nearly monochromatic Gobi. When she arrived at the airport with Rodion, he surprised her with his latest gift, which proved the most thoughtful: a pair of wraparound sunglasses that impressed her with how stylish she looked when checking herself out in the bathroom mirror. He and the professors were clear about her packing list, and she tossed in a pair of sunglasses, but these were so much cooler. Her backpack was bursting with gear, and it was suggested any electronics save her cell phone be left in Moscow. Whatever connectivity there would be on the expedition would be spotty at best. At least she could keep notes, take some personal pictures, and maybe play Wordl.

The flight from Moscow to Mongolia's capital city of Ulaanbaatar took just over six hours, and once you added delays in boarding and disembarking, it was nearly a seven-hour ordeal. She took advantage of the time to enjoy the creature comforts on the Aeroflot flight, which meant binging on movies and lots of Cool Cola.

After claiming their gear, they cleared Customs and she admired the new stamp in her passport. She never imagined being a world traveler until she was a full-fledged zoologist, but she didn't mind starting early. They were met by their guides, a husband-and-wife team who ushered them quickly into two trucks, the soldiers and gear in one, the scientists and interns in the other.

"What do you know about our destination?" Ella asked Sergei Lebedev, the oldest of the trio of scientists. He was entirely gray-haired with a neatly trimmed beard

"We're headed southwest, to the remotest part of the desert where the most sightings have been recorded," he said, his voice smoothly modulated, accustomed to lecturing, which she knew he had been doing for the last twenty years.

"Is there a chance the Death Worm is being mistaken for dinosaur fossils," she asked.

"My dear, while a great many fossils have been found — and have you had a chance to see the eggs we recovered? — we won't be near those digs. Honestly, Russia, or that is, the USSR, controlled the area and inhibited cultural and scientific investigations for decades. That all changed right before I joined the university in the early 1990s."

"But isn't the Death Worm a vertebrate so there's a misreading of bones?"

He blinked at that and shook his head. "No, my colleagues have managed to identify the bones uncovered to date, I doubt there would have been that sort of mistake."

"Are you doubting the existence of the worm?" Aleksandr Kozlov asked in a tone suggesting he didn't want her there.

Ella hesitated, uncertain how best to answer. Of course, she had her doubts. Despite a century's worth of written reports, there were decades of failed expeditions and no true evidence beyond oral history. She remained amazed the government would even foot the bill for a cryptid chase, uncertain why with such scant evidence. She didn't want to anger her hosts and needed their goodwill for future recommendations and networking opportunities. After all, Kozlov was a leading zoologist in Russia, author of nearly a dozen books on vertebrates. While that wasn't her specialty, he knew *everyone* in their field and could be an invaluable resource. He was ruggedly handsome with sandy brown hair and deep brown eyes. She settled on the middle ground, quoting one of her favorite films.

"I intend on keeping an open mind."

He grinned at that, showing yellow-stained teeth, that almost matched the yellowish nicotine stains on his hands.

"Smart girl."

Rodion glared at the exchange. She ignored him, refusing to let his attitude spoil her good mood.

"You know," Rodion interrupted, "the Death Worm likes it damp and is said to prefer coming out in the rain. But here's the complication: the rainy season is a joke. They get only 100 mm of rain annually, just inches at its peak. Compare that with the forty-three inches your Bucknell gets."

She blinked in surprise. He had bothered to learn a factoid to impress her. Ella flushed with warmth toward him, a rapid shift after the flash of annoyance she felt moments before. Could it be he used it to impress her or to use it as some argument for her to ditch Bucknell to stay in Moscow with him? She wouldn't have been surprised.

The trucks traveled for hours, covering hundreds of miles of rough, sunbaked roads. She periodically craned her neck to look at the steppes. Eventually, they gave way to desert sands, reflecting the sunlight, making her thankful for the new sunglasses.

"We have to be careful," Smirnov said, speaking for the first time since they left the airport. He'd spent the trip pouring over journals or tapping away at his solar-powered laptop, complete with satellite uplink, which Ella had learned was called the Sherpa 100AC, a hardened and tough-looking device, all gray, coupled to a Nomad 20 solar panel array. What wouldn't surprise her was that it was from the military stores, more typically taken into battle. On the other hand, if they found a Death Worm, it most certainly would put up a fight. "There has been reported a greater incidence of lizards in the area thanks to climate change. The weather extremes have altered migration and nesting patterns while desertification enlarges the Gobi, threatening the Chinese border."

"How close are we getting?" she asked.

"Close enough," he said without elaboration which concerned her but also made her thankful for the truckful of taciturn soldiers.

"More lizards, yes, but the plants are vanishing," Jargal Nergüi said in fluent Russian. She was maybe in her forties, her smooth, tight skin made it hard to tell. Her jet-black hair hung in bangs, peeking out from under the scarf she wore. Her teeth were a surprisingly brilliant white and there was some concern in those dark eyes.

"Meaning what?"

"My people use them for medicine," Jargal said. "More sand, more heat is making it hard to find what we need."

"She feels doomsday is coming," her husband, Chenghiz, added. He had a far more weathered face, deep lines like sand carving granite ran down his cheeks and across his forehead. He had a broad, square face, his skin a deeper bronze than his wife's. There was more merriment in his eyes, which Ella liked.

"It is. I hear the news. BBC, they don't lie," she snapped.

The couple had done work with other Russian researchers and had come recommended, but Rodion said no one knew much about them. In the end, they knew the territory and didn't object when the expedition's purpose was revealed. Jargal tried — unsuccessfully — to raise their fee upon hearing of their target, and continued to be bitter about it.

"You hear about the worm; do you believe in its existence?" Jargal challenged the professors.

Lebedev replied, "We are scientists. We hear about something, have some possible evidence, so we need to verify it. What about you?"

"I grew up on stories," she said. "My grandparents, my uncle, my neighbors. All have stories."

"But have you seen it?"

She kept her mouth closed, frowning.

"And you?" he asked Chenghiz.

"Like her, I was raised on stories," he said in a rough, phlegmy voice.

"So, maybe it does not exist," Kozlov said, earning disapproving looks from the others.

"We would be wasting precious time and our government's money," Lebedev said. Ella picked up a tone in his voice, uncertain what it was, but felt he might be hiding something.

There was a period of silence as the trucks ran over the rough roads, the miles and landscape passing by, seemingly unchanging. It was hot but not humid, still, Ella felt the perspiration begin on her back.

"Every culture has its stories," Rodion said, trying to be helpful. "Some have proven true, some not so much, and yet people believe. Like your Santa Claus."

"Hey, he's real," Ella said.

"Have you seen him?" he challenged.

"No, you're not supposed to. Are we not supposed to see the Death Worm?"

Their guides exchanged glances and Chenghiz shook his head slowly. "It is rarely above ground so the odds, the chances of being seen are small while the land is vast."

"We have our gods and we do not see them either," Jargal said.

Ella recalled in her hurried prep that the Mongolians were mostly Buddhists, and she was aware that meant a belief in spirits and gods, not anything monotheistic. Under the Communist rule, which ended only a few decades earlier, belief in anything had diminished but there was resurgence commensurate with the country's freedom.

"I would like to hear some of those stories," she told Jargal. The older woman made a dismissive sound and looked away.

"Those are best told on a full belly," Chenghiz said with a smile, trying to please his employers. "Something for later."

Ella nodded and smiled at him, trying to make friends, certain that would come in handy should things get tense. She already sensed some tension among their three leaders, and it was clear at least Chenghiz harbored some ill-will toward the soldiers, who must remind him of the bad old Soviet days.

"You want a story, how about one about the Yeti that killed Russian researchers in the Urals?" Lebedev said,

That caught her attention. "Wait, are Yetis real?"

"As real as the Death Worm," Chenghiz said.

She redirected her gaze to the scientist. "Tell me."

He shrugged; a mannerism seemingly universal to the men. "It was winter, 1959 and ten people from the Ural Polytechnic Institute went into the Gora Otorten mountains. After their two weeks were up and they hadn't returned, a rescue party was launched. They found two of them in only their socks and underwear. Later, they found three more near their tent. Four more were discovered in a ravine. Most of the corpses showed serious injuries, notably to their skulls and chests. It was a three-month investigation, quickly closed."

"Why?" she asked.

A shrug.

"And you think a Yeti attacked a camp of ten?"

Another shrug.

"Did anyone ever figure out what happened?"

"Nyet."

They rode on, the land a varying collection of beiges, tans, and browns, although the mountains in the distance threw darker shadows. Here and there, she spotted small clusters of circular white tents, and strings of camels leading other nomads who knew where. Now and then, she even spotted a motorcycle, the ubiquitous modern method of transport. Any time she saw anything resembling grasses, there were also flocks of sheep grazing in the summer heat. There were small ponds, nothing so grand as a lake, their placid surfaces reflecting the harsh sunlight.

This was to be her home for the next ten days and she had no clue how one sought the hidden prey that left no discernable tracks, no spoor to indicate presence. Thankfully, she was the junior member of the team, not expected to do more than observe, record, and experience. She was fine with that, but as the heat sent her to an unexpected nap, she also imagined a time she would be leading such expeditions, but promised herself her target would be something tangible.

When Ella awoke after dreaming of worms and yetis, the trucks had paused, letting those who needed to relieve themselves do so, although there were no outhouses. The soldiers merely wandered away from the trucks, turned their backs, and let fly. She wondered what Jargal or the female soldier, Haajar Turgenev, were expected to do. Apparently, it involved walking even further away and squatting. That was most unappealing, but she might have to shed some sense of modesty on the trip, because there was no way she could hold it for a week.

The sun was dipping toward the horizon, and she was told there were another few hours to go before they reached the first stop on their hunt. Apparently, their guides had been there prior to the flight landing, preparing it for their guests, which she was thankful for. Despite the nap, she was still tired and didn't relish the notion of building their version of a tent in the dark. Still, they had a few hours of travel and she didn't like the idea; her butt ached, her back was sore, and without a cell signal, she couldn't check her social media. It was clear their road stopped being a traditional paved surface, transitioning to something rougher, less finished, certainly not paved. The jarring increased with every mile, but no one was thrown from their seats. For her, this was going to be a real lesson in "roughing it," no creature comforts and plenty of hard work just to live off the land.

Just when she thought she'd go out of her mind with boredom, given the lack of conversation offered by her companions, the trucks began to slow and finally stopped. Smirnov hopped out first, followed by Chenghiz and Jargal. There were some other sounds as the soldiers piled out, but what truly caught Ella's attention was the aroma. Roasting meat over a fire. Suddenly, her mouth watered, and she realized how hungry she was. The snack bars since leaving the airport did little to satisfy her and she was ravenous. At least this meant getting out and getting fed, without first having to build a tent. For this, she would thank whichever deity Jargal recommended.

There were four broad, white yurts, which she was told were called ger, circling a sizeable campfire. There were two teen Mongolians tending the fire, over which hung a roasting hunk of meat on a spit. They clearly had prepared their meal in advance, awaiting the visitors. Smirnov exchanged some words with Chenghiz and then poked his head in, waving for everyone to come out. It had been some time since Ella had the freedom of movement and was thrilled to stretch her back out and move merely. Once she twisted around, loosening up, she took in the campground. Tethered to some sort of post were several camels, silent witnesses to the human activity. There was nothing but the fire and four ger—no electric wires, streetlights, or even sounds beyond soft voices and grease dripping into the fire, crackling on contact. So remote. She could have been on another world given how different it was from Virginia.

Rodion walked over and handed her a mug, warm to the touch. It smelled vaguely like tea, and she took a tentative sip. It was sweeter than she liked and realized there was milk present. He clinked mugs with her and said with a broad grin, "Welcome to the real Mongolia!"

She grinned back. She truly was on an adventure.

They walked over to the others as Ella adjusted to the odd-tasting tea. Others had hauled their backpacks out of the trucks and placed them in their ger, following Jargal's direction. The five soldiers were directed to one ger while the scientists and interns were placed in another. That left one for the guides, and one for the helpers. These were identified from the outside, with a domed top rising to about six feet high with a tall, thin chimney. Each had a brightly decorated door, ornately painted with distinctive signs, denoting the occupants of each to avoid confusion. Rodion led her into one opposite the fire and she was glad no one was very tall, because the ceiling felt low, giving an initial impression of a confined space. In truth, the tent was wide and spacious, with a rectangular iron stove in the center, designed for individual family meal preparation. Where the exterior was plain, colorful rugs hung from the wooden frames of the interior. Small dressers and a worktable were in one section. Another had prayer rugs atop the carpeted flooring. She was surprised by how much wool went into the flooring, wall coverings, and other elements, but then again, from a country dependent on sheep for everything, their wool came in rather handy. There were four sleeping mats clustered together to the west of the door while a single mat waited for her in the kitchen area, to the east. Well, sexism remained a Mongolian tradition.

It was warm in the space, despite the bottoms being rolled up to let the cooling evening airflow. She was thankful the stove was not in use.

Jargal was directly behind Ella and spoke up. "You enter and go left. Always. Never walk between the pillars."

"Why?" she asked.

"Bad luck," Jargal spat out. Then she added, "Old men sit opposite the door, you on either side. To the north is also where you pray."

Ella took it all in, recognizing there were no interior walls, no privacy of any sort so that was going to be interesting.

"Come, eat," Jargal ordered.

Outside, everyone clustered around the fire, happy to be standing after all this time. The guides and their helpers made plates filled with lamb, cheese, and cheese curds. As each plate was filled, it was handed to someone, complete with a napkin and utensils. When a plate was handed to her, Ella nodded thanks and let the enticing aroma of the seasoned meat fill her nostrils. She would rather sit to eat, but no one else did, so she remained standing. The meat was tender, having cooked long, and the spices used were unfamiliar to her. Her first few bites were to satisfy her hunger then she slowed and savored each mouthful, trying to identify the blend of seasonings, wishing she knew more about cooking.

Once the party had food, the helpers, young boys, maybe early teens, rushed about bringing everyone mugs with a fermented milk beer. The soldiers practically guzzled their cups, but it tasted terrible to her. The silent teens withdrew once they were done serving, hustling over to the trucks, where they unloaded a series of solar panels, which would be essential in the coming days.

The soldiers kept to themselves, telling bawdy jokes and embarrassing stories, finally able to relax. Rodion and Ella stood near the scientists, who were examining everything they could see, from the star arrangements to the fading sunlight and dropping temperatures. It was clinical and not terribly interesting.

"Do you really think we'll be successful where so many have failed," she finally asked during a lull in the dull conversation.

Smirnov looked down his long nose at her, black brows knit together. "You wish us to fail?"

She recoiled at the accusation. "No, I ask purely from a scientific standpoint. It's been a century of writings but no photographic evidence. Just the remains of something no one can quite identify, your predecessors ignored that for decades."

"Miss Trigiani," Smirnov began in a tone that suggested he was accustomed to lecturing those he considered to be idiots. "When Europeans first traveled to Africa, they had never seen apes and gorillas before. They returned home with fantastical stories about a continent filled with black people and monsters. Some stories even merged the two. Lions. Zebra. Emu. These were all strange to the untrained eyes of explorers. Today, they are all mammals under your watchful gaze, am I correct?"

She nodded, biting her tongue at his tone.

"Scientists around the world are still making new discoveries even though we have filled every nook and cranny of this planet with people. We continue to make new finds each year. Aleks, what was it you were going on about on the flight?"

"The nano-chameleon," his colleague answered. "This is now considered the smallest reptile known to man. It is barely larger than a fingernail. And it doesn't alter its coloring, unlike its namesake."

Okay, that was interesting. But it also started the three on a can-you-top-this list of recent discoveries, from the Emperor Dumbo Octopus to the African Bright Orange Bat, a find Ella had heard about, it being a mammal. She had to concede their point, rephrasing.

"What will we do differently from previous expeditions to improve our odds?"

"Good question," Rodion said, trying to be supportive despite the professors' collective disdain.

"That it is, Rodion," Lebedev agreed. "We are trying not to be arrogant enough to presume we know what we're doing here. Instead, we let those who grew up on the stories lead us to the likeliest places to spot the worm or evidence. We'll be setting up cameras to record designated spots, and we will follow the experts." His hand gestured toward their guides, who were finishing their meals.

"What makes them experts," Rodion asked.

"When we received approval for this expedition, I reached out to colleagues at the universities here and asked for guides well-versed on the Death Worm and where to find it."

"They took you seriously?" Ella asked, instantly regretting the question, but it was out.

"They did," Korlov confirmed. "Like us, they would like to find evidence once and for all to settle the question. We may have known about it for a century, but they've lived with the stories for millennia."

"Better we try to find it and fall, victim, proving the truth of the matter, than risk their fellow countrymen," Smirnov said darkly. The others laughed.

Ella remained skeptical, uncertain why they thought they could succeed if, after thousands of years, no true evidence had ever been produced. But she finished her meal, sipping gingerly at the horrid beer, and let the thoughts fade into the back of her mind.

In a display of gallantry, the men insisted Ella enter their ger first and prepare for bed, signaling when it was proper for them to enter. She wondered idly how long this would last. The entire contingent was tired and would be turning in early, which was fine by her, knowing they'd be up with the sun. Ella rushed through her nighttime routine and then lay down in a t-shirt and shorts, placing a thin woven blanket over her, remembering to sleep with her feet toward the door and not the altar. Still, she felt her body relax as her mind turned over exactly why they were there, how they would succeed, and what it would mean if they did. She studied the dim poles holding up their ger, slowly starting to count them to shove other thoughts from her mind. She never made it past eighteen.

The following morning, Ella stepped outside of the ger dressed in layers, looking forward to breaking in her new lightweight hiking boots. Wearing a pale green long-sleeve shirt over a t-shirt, dun-colored pants, and a floppy hat over her tied-back hair, she felt refreshed and ready to go out into the steppes or the desert and find the Mongolian Death Worm. Glancing around the encampment, she saw Chenghiz standing alone across the way, studying the terrain as if divining where to begin the day's hunt.

"Good morning," she said in Russian.

He nodded. "Let me teach you our greeting. You can say, Sain bain uu? It's your 'how do you do?'"

She repeated it, mangling the final word so he repeated it a few times as she practiced until he finally nodded in approval.

"Thank you."

"To be less formal, you may say, Sen-ooo, which is 'hello'."

Ella repeated the phrase and got it right the first time, earning her a broad smile of approval.

"What else can I teach you today?"

"I didn't know class was in session."

"We are always learning," he said, sounding more like a cleric than a tour guide, but she appreciated the sentiment.

"Well, I counted eighty-one poles as I tried to fall asleep last night. Is that typical?"

"Having trouble sleeping?" he said with a smile.

"No, the poles. Are gers identical?"

"Eighty-one is a multiple of nine, a sacred number to us," he replied. "There are some bigger ones, but we use this size."

"Are they complicated to erect?"

"Not really, you learn as you grow up since everyone helps. These take about three hours apiece to put together and we always build them so the door faces south. When taken down, they roll up nicely and everything can be tied to a camel when we move on."

"Wow, that's very specific."

"Most everything is," he said with some gravity. "Everything should have a meaning. Our culture has many beliefs, and we honor them through the centuries. You see the chimney?"

She nodded.

"The opening around it is designed to act as a portal to the world above. It is connected by the stovepipe to the stove, which represents the five basic elements: earth, wood, fire, metal, and water. It is also our portal to the world below."

"What else should I know?

"Hmm. We do not knock on doors as you do. You just enter."

"Even if I am getting dressed?"

He smiled and nodded causing her to flush.

"And do not linger in the doorway. Enter to speak with someone or do it from outside. Now, come eat." He began to move toward the center of camp where others were gathering.

"What's for breakfast?"

"Milk tea, boortsog—fried dough to you, and urum, clotted cream. Eat and then we begin your hunt."

Ella wasn't sure about the tea; it was salted and not to her liking, but she could not be rude. Rodion already warned her it was impolite not to finish one's plate. To top it off, she wasn't all that hungry, chalking it up to the day before. In fact, she was feeling *off*, ascribing it to the heat. But she needed to eat because it promised to be a long, hot day. The salt was also probably a good thing, given their perspiration. It was already warm, and she wished for iced water to bring along but that wasn't going to happen. Instead, everyone had canteens over their shoulders or in backpacks. The soldiers looked ready for combat, armed with pistols and rifles in addition to their other gear. She took cold comfort in the fact that such protection existed, even if it cast an unsavory sheen over the expedition.

Jargal was not far from them, finishing readying a collection of horses that had been delivered overnight. The trucks were also gone, to return in ten days to collect everyone. No one asked if she had ever ridden before, it was just assumed by her hosts. Thankfully, this was not her first time, but it had been maybe fifteen years, so she would have to get accustomed all over again. She found herself looking forward to riding a horse across the desert, much as explorers had centuries before, a chance to feel what they felt.

"Ready?"

Rodion's question startled her from her reverie and she nodded vigorously. He stole a kiss, tasting the salty milk, and grinned expansively at the horizon. "This is going to be a great day."

"You sound like we're going to find the worm today. Are you that confident?"

"Nah, but it's all about the mindset. We *will* find it and that hunt begins now."

"Where are we headed?"

"Southeast. Chenghiz checked with the people making the horse delivery and apparently it rained over that direction yesterday."

"How far?"

He shrugged. "A few hours, perhaps. Ready to be Lawrence of Arabia?"

"I don't know if you noticed, but I'm a girl," Ella said.

"Oh, that I have noticed, dushka."

Smirnov waved them over and everyone gathered, the first time the entire contingent stood side by side, focused on their goal. He showed them a paper relief map of the region and said the ride would take three to four hours, probably with breaks for the heat. Once they arrived, they would begin surveying. He outlined proper protocols for the soldiers so as not to spoil evidence.

"If you see something, anything that is anomalous, signal one of us. Touch nothing because if it is the worm, their acid can be deadly."

"So is touching them," Jargal added.

"Old wives' tale," Chenghiz chided.

"I *am* an old wife, so yes, deadly," she shot back.

"If you see something, signal us. If you hear something, signal us. No one should be solo," Smirnov said.

"Even if I have to take a shit?" asked Valerik Belyaev, a bored-looking soldier whose very demeanor signaled he'd seen it all before and was world-weary.

Ella rolled her eyes but noticed Kozlov had been staring at her, clearly wondering if she needed the same instructions the soldiers received. She'd show him, prove her worth. How had yet to be determined but clearly, he needed to be shown she wouldn't be a hindrance.

Thankfully, Smirnov ignored the question and accompanying snickers. Instead, he looked around and decided a pep talk was needed.

"We're here at great expense because finding this worm has been deemed of great scientific value. While all scientific research has importance, new discoveries are vital. We may not get wealthy from this, we may not all get our names in the newspapers, but we will be part of some momentous. To be successful, we must be both alert and wary. You are all here because your expertise is valued. You all have roles, so fulfill them, support and protect one another, and this will be a successful expedition."

"At least here they still read the newspaper," Ella whispered to Rodion.

"Shush, he's making a speech," he whispered back, not taking his eyes off the man. She rolled her own eyes.

She'd heard worse and certain she'd heard better, but it seemed to transition them from travelers to explorers. There were murmurs of assent, nods of heads, and then with a clucking of his tongue, Chenghiz led the group to their horses. Rodion offered to help her up, but Ella shot him a look and he backed off with a grin. Ella was surprised at how much smaller the Mongolian horses were than the ones she was used to back home. Hers was a medium brown, with powerful-looking forequarters, and a thick, strong neck. She was amazed at how wide the body was and was afraid she'd develop sore muscles from hours of riding, but it had to be endured. He seemed good-natured and quiet, letting her climb up without moving, his thick black tail gently swaying a bit.

"What's he named?"

"We do not name our horses," Chenghiz said. "We call them by their color."

"That's so impersonal," she said, stroking the neck, feeling the corded muscles. The ears twitched in reaction but didn't move to object. "Can I call him Chestnut?"

"Is that a color?"

"Yes."

"Yes."

Once everyone secured their gear and mounted, Jargal rode by them, one-by-one, nodding in approval or making minute adjustments. As she finished, she took the lead, and the posse headed out. No one talked, taking in the sights, getting used to their mounts' movements. Chestnut didn't sway, walking sure-footed and giving Ella confidence.

"These horses have not changed much, if at all, since Genghis Khan," Chenghiz told her as he pulled up to ride side-by-side. At least someone was taking a liking to her, other than Rodion that was. "My people can trace the horses back some 4000 years. This breed—the Gobi—has proven influential, I am told, around the world."

"Well, that's impressive," she said. Her imagination now stretched to try and picture being part of Khan's army, conquering Asia one mile at a time. How powerful he must have been and how influential given the legends that still surround him today.

"He likes you," Chenghiz said.

"Chestnut? How can you tell?"

"His body language. As he gets used to you will be able to see for yourself."

She thought about that and then turned to the mission. "Do you think we will find the Death Worm?"

"I don't know what to think. Jargal is certain of its existence, and she is no fool. I would like the matter to be settled by scientists. Too many tourists come and hope to find it then leave disappointed. Certainty would be nice."

"Oh, I agree with that," she said.

The riding was pleasant enough despite the rising sun and with it the temperature. Everyone tried to pace their drinking and as the perspiration began to bother her, Ella rolled up her sleeves. She'd added a kerchief around her neck, thankful for the gifted sunglasses as they helped cut the daylight glare. Other than the *clip-clop* of the horses' unshod hooves, no other sound could be heard. The steppe was starting to mix with the sand, the dreaded, fabled Gobi Desert coming into focus. Already, she saw dunes on the horizon, mountains behind them, the land getting more golden. Part of her thrilled to it, part of her dreaded the enduring heat. Four hours to the first spot, four hours back, and who knew how many hours looking for a fable. This could get tedious fast, but she doubted anyone wanted to sing "100 Bottles of Beer on the Wall."

By the second hour, Ella's thighs started to burn from straddling the horse, but it wasn't his fault. Chestnut proved sure-footed as they left the steppe into the desert, the hard-packed pathways flanked by endless sand, golden and white in the hot sun. The vista shifted to an endless sea of sand, stretching to the horizon, the uneven shapes of hills and dunes keeping things from being purely monotonous. Most of the others spoke little so she focused on the scenery, uncertain as to what they would find.

As the fourth hour arrived, they had stopped just once. Sore and sweaty, Ella wondered if she'd made a mistake in agreeing to this "adventure." Chenghiz and Jargal seemed unfazed by their trek, leading the ten other horses in single-file, more or less. The terrain was sandy and rocky, with no discernable signs of life, be it human, animal, or cryptid. She wanted to ask, "Are we there yet?" but refused to sound like a child. Already the youngest member of the team, Ella didn't want to call attention to that. She was therefore thankful when the leaders slowed their gait, forcing everyone to follow suit. They had crested a rise in the land and obviously saw something. Lebedev urged his horse ahead of the others to join their guides. Behind her, Ella could hear some mumbles from the soldiers which was an improvement over the grumbles she had picked up throughout the journey.

The scientist gestured for Smirnov and Kozlov to join the others at the rise and now Ella felt the stirrings in her chest, the now-alert thrill of discovery eager to emerge. She doubted it was the Death Worm itself, but she hoped for evidence. Finally, there was a general wave without urgency so gingerly, she dismounted, patting Chestnut's neck in thanks, and stretched a bit. By that point, Rodion came up beside her. Exchanging curious and excited glances, they hurried ahead to join their leaders.

There was a moment of crushing disappointment as she climbed up the small rise and looked down to see not a Death Worm, but half-buried animal bones. They had been bleached by sand, wind, and sun, turning them blindingly white in contrast to the sand. She squinted a bit against the glare and tried to discern what type of animal it was.

"So, my student, what is it?" Smirnov said to Rodion.

"May I?" He gestured to get closer, and Chenghiz waved him forward. There was absolutely nothing threatening in the vicinity, not from what Ella could tell, and she realized how disappointed she was feeling at the moment.

Rodion carefully worked his way down the rise, slipping on the loose sand, but he quickly gained his balance and approached the bones. He squatted low and examined them from several angles without touching. With a small camera from his backpack, he took several pictures, always recording the evidence.

"So?" Smirnov asked.

"I believe it's an ibex," he announced.

Both Ella and Kozlov made disapproving sounds. That caused Smirnov to whirl about and challenge the student.

"Why not?"

"May I?" Ella interrupted, imitating her boyfriend. Without waiting for approval, she worked her way to Rodion's side. Like him, she got low and looked at multiple angles before pointing to a femur.

"It's too large to be an ibex. They grow less than four feet high but look at the length of the femur. That alone suggests it stood at least seven feet tall. That would make it the wild ass."

From above, Smirnov applauded with approval.

She felt validated which proved fleeting when Rodion glowered behind his sunglasses. Clearly, his male pride had been wounded. But she had studied the Gobi wildlife on the flight, he didn't.

Before she could say something, the ground beneath her shifted with her weight, and she tumbled forward into the skeleton. She sprawled across it, slicing open her forearm against something jagged. Scrambling to her feet, she bit her tongue to avoid letting out a cry of pain. Blood streamed down her arm, drunk by the hard, dry ground.

"Damn it," Rodion said loudly. "Medic!"

Grisha Preobrazhensky, the soldier with emergency medical training, hurried forward down the slope, reaching for his fluorescent green medical kit at the same time. Ella stood there, cradling her injured arm, and cursed herself for her lack of caution. The last thing she wanted was to be a hindrance.

Preobrazhensky reached her quickly, snapped open the case, and then proceeded to examine and treat the wound. Quickly, he withdrew gauze and antiseptic cream. Some of the gauze was used to wipe away the blood, and he sighed in relief, telling her, "It's not deep." He worked efficiently, cleaning, disinfecting, and then carefully wrapping the injured forearm within minutes.

Ella thanked the man, who was stocky and seemed built like a human tank yet worked with a deftness that she didn't expect.

She studied his gear as he put away the supplies and was somewhat surprised by what she saw.

"Duct tape?"

"When in doubt, it fixes most things," he said with a grin. "And when that fails, I use super kley."

"Seriously?"

"Sure. First aid is more than bandages and aspirin," he said, indicating the assortment of supplies. She spotted a suture stapler, digital thermometer, even nail clippers. Then she reached over and withdrew a package.

"Condoms?"

"It is best to be prepared for all contingencies," he said, then rummaged lower to withdraw a thin cardboard box. She recognized the iconography even if she couldn't read the Cyrillic letters: a pregnancy test kit. They shared smiles at the even-handedness of the gear and she admired just how prepared he was. She was just sorry she had to be the first to require his skill. But now she knew she could rely on him regardless of what came next.

As he closed the lid, she returned her gaze to the skeleton, curious as to what she cut herself on. Rodion apparently had the same question as he was studying the bones, taking pictures, and even some measurements. She came close to him, giving him a reassuring smile.

"You in pain?"

"Not really and if I was, he probably has the best drugs. So, what do you see?"

He pointed to the exposed portion of the rib cage, which was now dotted with her blood. Some of it dripped from the bones, but others settled in depressions which she knew shouldn't be there. Withdrawing a pair of gloves from his backpack, Rodion took a cloth to wipe away the blood and it was clear now that the ribs were scarred in some way, creating rough edges where she cut herself.

"What is it?" Kozlov called from above.

"Some unusual scarring on the ribs," Rodion replied.

That caught the man's attention. He worked his way down to join them, carrying a magnifying glass in one latex-gloved hand. The others parted to allow him to get close and examine it in detail. He ran the glass close to the bones. Slowly, he worked from rib to rib, then scraped away some of the sand around it, exposing more of the rib cage, and gestured for Rodion to take additional pictures. He happily snapped away, leaving Ella feeling useless, her forearm slightly throbbing from the bandage.

"So, Rodion, what do you think?"

"Animal attack? Fighting asses?"

"Like my students in class," the older man said, letting out a rough laugh. "Maybe. What about you, Ella?"

"Maybe," she conceded.

"You think something else did this?"

"Look at the ribs and imagine what animal native to the region could have done this? It would have to have been something with strong claws or antlers. Two come to mind: the snow leopard, but this isn't its environment; or the Gobi Bear."

"But there are fewer than three dozen we know of," Rodion protested. "The odds of a bear attacking the ass makes no sense. They're herbivores."

"Right," she agreed.

"Acid," Kozlov said quietly. "The Death Worm's acid could have caused this kind of damage."

Rodion and Ella exchanged surprised glances before locking eyes with the professor, who seemed serious.

He met their skepticism with a question. "What else could have caused this damage?"

Ella had no answers but needed more information. She cocked her head toward the skeleton, and Rodion got her message. Together, using the tools from his backpack, they excavated carefully, exposing more of the skeleton, which was, fortunately, only shallowly buried by the elements. they shifted the sand away, exposing decomposing fur and muscle. The remains showed the same pattern of yellowish discoloration as the damaged ribs. The more of the ass they uncovered, the more overwhelming the odor of decomposition grew in the desert heat, but Ella didn't pause to cover her nose, even as her stomach did a flip. It was difficult work, and she felt like a hot mess: her thighs still burned, she ached from the injury, plus now she sweated profusely. She dared not appear weak. Not on the first day. Not ever. Those leading the search held no patience for weakness. This was the work she signed up and she would make the most of the opportunity.

After fifteen minutes, enough was exposed for Kozlov to take additional photos. He withdrew a specimen vial and scraped off some of the discolored fur and offal inside. With a satisfying pop, the lid locked in place. He hastily scribbled a note on the label already affixed.

"Our first piece of evidence, not bad for day one, eh?"

The others nodded and followed him back up the slope to the rest of the expedition, who had all gathered to watch the work being done. As they reached the top, Chenghiz handed Ella a canteen, which she wanted to swallow whole, but sipped slowly. Kozlov recounted their findings and his suppositions, receiving a mix of nods and stares. Only Jargal smiled with a sense of vindication. Chenghiz let everyone else chat and drink as he scanned their surroundings and then went down the slope to examine the find for himself. He walked around the carcass, stood with his back to it, and looked out. Finally, he climbed the slope and joined the others.

"What did you see?" Lebedev asked.

Chenghiz gestured in the direction of the dead ass. "It rained in this area a day or two ago, which is why that poor thing was here, hunting for food in the scrub. But look to the right. Do you see those patterns?"

The old scientist craned his neck in the direction indicated, a hand over his eyes, then slowly nodded. "What made them?"

"Not the wind or rain," he replied.

"Those were intentionally made?"

"If your conclusion is that the Death Worm killed that creature, then it came from that direction," Chenghiz said.

Ella overheard the exchange, stunned at the possibilities being discussed. Had they truly found evidence of a Mongolian Death Worm? Were they that close? She kept those questions to herself, but from the sounds behind her, it was clear she wasn't the only one to hear the exchange.

"So, my friend, where do go from here?"

Chenghiz considered the question, continuing to scan the desert, divining an answer.

"It is gone," he finally said. "There's nothing for it here. We go back to the camp to consult the laptop. I need to see where it might rain next and take you there."

Just like that, the find was now history as they saddled up and began the long ride back to their camp. As she rode, Ella cataloged her aches and pains, wondering how she'd be feeling on day ten. Still, her heart beat strongly as she thrilled to the idea that she was in the Gobi, making contributions, and actually on the trail of… something. This made her feel alive and excited about what tomorrow might reveal.

CHAPTER FOUR

As it turned out, days two and three proved to be incredibly disappointing. When they had returned to the camp, their guides consulted maps courtesy of their satellite phone, making calls to check a meteorologist they regularly consulted. They used their maps to indicate possible courses where rainfall was expected over the next week, but they cautioned that each shower would be brief and to a degree unpredictable. As a result, they warned, there was no guarantee they'd arrive in time before the arid air greedily sucked away the moisture.

Most everyone had been euphoric that their first day resulted in something conclusive. The soldiers equated the lack of a genuine answer to the corpse's death to the existence of the Death Worm. After all, the learned scientists had ruled out all other answers. The scientists and interns were certainly heartened by the discovery and evidence to be analyzed back in Russia. Still, they were cautious in their optimism, lacing equivocating words into their statements, refusing to let the soldiers lull them into sloppy thinking.

Ella, for her part, was delighted at any kind of a find but continued to have her doubts. She nursed those, along with her injury, on the next two outings, long, arduous rides that revealed nothing. They had gone deeper into the desert, at an angle from where the carcass was found, but there was nothing, not even a suspicious ripple in the sand.

On the third day, they skirted the base of some mountains, their sparse shadows leaving damp spots from rain that ended before they arrived. Smaller lizards and snakes were seen in the mud. She took some delight in spotting a Marbled Polecat climb the rocks high above her. Watching, she saw it snatch a small bird that dared to land on an outcropping too close to the hungry animal.

The long rides were tedious, the conversation halting at best, but by then, the scientists and soldiers had finally relaxed around one another. They debated sports and arts, even daring to get into politics with gentle complaints about the current regime and its excesses. She was pleased that the more common ground found among the travelers the deeper the bonds of trust they formed. Ella formed a good rapport with Chenghiz, who acted as a father figure, talking about life as a nomad, how to read the skies and desert, how to tend to the animals.

His advice on the first day helped her to bond with Chestnut. On the second morning, it reacted to her approach, nuzzling her, eating the oats she proffered in her left hand. She felt more comfortable riding him and would come to miss him when it was time to fly back to Moscow. It turned out, Chestnut loved being brushed, so she made time for it morning and evening.

The food and fermented drink still were not to her taste. In fact, the mere aroma made her queasy. She ate because she had to, sipped when she needed to, especially with a limited amount of water. As a result, each night she found herself thinking about the rich, flavorful foods she would gorge on once back in Moscow. When she first arrived, it was all too rich for her, too much sauce and gravy, but she had come to like it, especially once Rodion began showing her his favorites.

Still feeling a little weak and a little hungry, no doubt connected, Ella sat around the fire as the sun cast silhouettes on the faraway horizon. Several of the soldiers had drunk her share of the alcoholic milk drink and then some, so they felt no pain despite complaining earlier of saddle sores. There was more than a little complaining about the lack of progress after the first day's excitement, causing Lebedev to snap at the quintet, reminding them they were warned nothing may come of it at all so their find was better than anticipated. That mollified them, for now at least.

"How are you?" she heard the English in a thick voice. Ella turned to see Grisha Preobrazhensky approach, a half-empty cup of alcohol in his hand.

"Fine, thank you," she replied, still in English.

"That is good. How about those Yankees?"

She chuckled at that. "I don't know, I am a Nationals fan. What do you know about the Yankees?"

"Nothing," he admitted, squatting beside her, his bulk dwarfing her. "They play beysbol, yes?"

"Base. Ball. And yes."

"Baseball," he repeated, beaming when she gave him a thumb's up. "What are Nationals?"

"There are two leagues, the American and the National. The Yankees, one of the game's oldest teams, is in the American League. My team, the Washington Nationals, relocated from Montreal, Canada and play in the National League."

"American. National. So similar."

"Yes, they are. Patriotic."

"Being a patriot is not always easy," he said.

"Being a patriot is easier than understanding the infield fly rule."

The medic blinked in confusion. "The what?"

"It's a game rule. Never mind. Have you been studying English long," she asked.

"Two years," he said. "For me to advance, I need to be mnogoyazychnyy... many languages."

"Multilingual," she said.

"Da."

"What sort of advancement do you want?"

"Czar would be nice, but the job no longer exists." He let out a long breath. "I serve now but want to attend medical school, be a doctor."

"I approve," she said with a smile.

"Language is hard," he said.

"No, Russian is hard, English is just slozhnyy."

"Very true. May I practice with you during this mission?"

"Please. I need to stay sharp, too," she said. Finally, she was making friends, and having a soldier on her side didn't hurt. He was kinder and gentler, it seemed, than Rodion, whose bluster continued even out here in the desert.

Later, Rodion huddled against her, leaning into her which she appreciated considering there was zero privacy. Kisses and groping had been quick and hidden, making her relive her high school days, which brought back a mix of emotions. He offered her some of his drink, but she wrinkled her nose at it and just sat quietly.

"Tell us a story," Fredek Bortnik, one of the soldiers, called to their guides.

Jargal shrugged and got closer to the fire, seemingly considering the options. "You want this Death Worm so much; let me tell you of one such encounter. I heard it from my cousin when I was a child. There was a young boy, playing outside when he encountered a yellow toy box, one he had never seen before. Curious, he picked it up, shaking it to see if it made music. When it didn't, he opened the lid and a young Death Worm lay inside. Thinking he found a pet of some sort, the boy reached to touch it, but as his fingers grazed the red skin, he convulsed and fell over dead."

She paused, her eyes going around the fire to ensure everyone listened.

"The dead boy's parents came outside to find his body and how they shrieked. They cursed themselves and then saw the yellow-tinged fingers. They saw a wavy trail in the ground near the box, heading toward the sand. The grieving father grabbed a farm tool and followed the trail, intent on killing it. The wife stayed behind, wailing on her knees. In time, she dried her eyes and realized her husband had not returned. She went off to follow the trail and saw her husband dead, one hand and part of his face melted away from the worm's acid spray."

There was silence except for the crackle of the fire.

"Are all your stories about the Death Worm," Fredek Bortnik slurred. "Have you got nothing else to talk about?"

Chenghiz cleared his throat and spoke. "We have a rich history, my friend. Name something, and I am sure we have a story for you."

"Camels," Haajar Turgenev called out. The others cheered drunkenly.

"Camels it is. Listen and learn why camels roll in ashes."

"They do?" she asked.

"In my story they do. You see, a long time ago, Sakamuni Borhan..." he began before Jargal interrupted.

"Sakamuni Buddha, who was the first god to the idolaters," she said in explanation, not that it helped Ella, who studied Mongolian animals to prepare for the expedition not mythology. Still, she was fascinated.

"Quite so. Now, Bohran was naming the months of our calendar, naming each month after a different animal. He had finished with eleven and realized there was one month but two animals — the rat and the camel. Each argued the month should bear its name. Bohran, wise as he was, could not decide, nor did he wish either to be upset. He asked them to decide between themselves and he would honor their choice.

"Well, the camel and the rat decided that whichever first saw the rays of the following morning's sun would have the honor of being the twelfth month. Now, the camel was wise and experienced. He lived in the desert and knew how the sun would rise in the east, so he stood, gazing at the horizon through the night, awaiting the new day.

"The rat, for its part, climbed his opponent and settled on the hump, facing the mountains to the west. He fixed his eyes on the mountaintop. As happens each day, the sun began to appear, casting its light, catching the top of the mountain before clearing the horizon.

"Outsmarted, the camel was unhappy to lose to a small rat, so he shook the rat to the ground and tried to stomp it to death with his hooves. The rat avoided those hooves and hid in a pile of ashes.

"To this day, whenever a camel sees a place where ashes have been scattered, such as we do in the morning, he wishes revenge and first stops, then drops and rolls in the ashes, hoping to crush the rat. Each camel follows this practice, and each camel finds itself disappointed."

Several soldiers clapped at the tale.

"You, sir, have proven your point. Well done," Haajar admitted, hoisting her cup high in salute.

There were more stories and talk as the night settled among them. By then, several stood and mingled. Ella and Grisha had gotten into a talk about hiking, something she was unaccustomed to and something he adored, hence his being the best prepared of the soldiers. There was a touch of pride in the boast, enough that those around him cheered and drank some more. By then, most were drunk and Lebedev had already turned in. Rodion and the other two scientists were chatting with Jargal as Chenghiz policed the area, happily singing to himself.

"How much longer will you be in Russia," Grisha asked her in English.

"I leave August 12," she said.

"Good," he said before switching back to Russian, "then there will be time for me to show you what good hiking is. Not this desert, but something prettier and cooler. I will take you on the Lavra trail where you can visit the monastery at Trinity Lavra of St. Sergius. It dates to the 14th century, and I find it quite beautiful and peaceful."

By then, he had looped his arm with hers as they walked the perimeter and he went on about the trail. He was definitely flirting or even hitting on her, but he was charming in his own way, drunk enough not to remember she was with Rodion.

As he discussed the beautiful sights, the sound of rushing footsteps approached and then Rodion was there, in front of both. He looked furious and swung a fist at Grisha, glancing off the man's ear.

"What the hell are you doing?" the medic roared, rushing Rodion, grabbing him around the waist and tackling him to the ground. By then, the others had rushed over with Timor Yegorov and Nicolai Smirnov pulling them apart. Timor shoved Grisha away, toward their ger, yelling at him so rapidly Ella had trouble translating the invective. She turned her attention to Rodion, who was breathing hard, brushing dirt off his clothes. A part of her was pleased he was there to defend her honor, which felt very old school to her.

"What are you doing letting that dog put his hands all over you?" he barked.

And there it was, the semi-neanderthal throwback attitude, blaming her for Grisha's actions. At that moment, she was furious with him and with herself for liking any part of the incident. He stalked to the ger and she hesitated to follow, really hating the lack of privacy it offered. They'd confront one another, in front of their superiors, and it could get ugly. She chose, instead, to walk the perimeter, despite how tired she felt, allowing herself to calm down and, hopefully, allowing Rodion to fall asleep. This way, she could return without incident. At least until the morning.

CHAPTER FIVE

It already promised to be a hot uncomfortable day when Ella awoke, feeling tired, and not looking forward to another fruitless trek. Still, this was what she signed up for and she had damn well better get used to the life of an explorer in the field if that was her real desire. What she was less certain about as she brushed her teeth, ignoring the stirrings around her, was what to do about Rodion. He infuriated her with his attitudes, his sense of entitlement to her. But he was also funny, smart, and could be very kind. In a way, she rationalized, last night's scuffle was a demonstration of his love. It just didn't meet her ideal partner profile and she had to come to terms with that.

Again, she wondered why he had to fight Grisha, but that diverted her mind to think more about the presence of five soldiers. That felt excessive to her if all they were there for was mere protection. She'd heard nothing of vandals or human dangers so, to her mind, they were two or three soldiers too many.

When she emerged from the ger for breakfast, she was assaulted by the smell of cooking meat, even at this hour. They ate meat, usually lamb, for their meals day and night so the idea of muesli or a bagel was beyond their understanding. Thankfully, she wasn't too hungry and would just have some bread and dried fruit. Anything salted was definitely unappealing.

Rodion had emerged quietly behind her and kept his distance, as did Grisha, who stayed huddled with his mug of tea, talking with Fredek and Haajar. Everyone spoke in subdued tones, ensuring nothing volatile would happen. As it was, Rodion gave her a half-hearted apology and she made him go shake hands with Grisha to disperse the tension before they set off into the arid day. The three professors, for their part, ignored it all, preferring to chat with Jargal about their path for the fourth day. Within the hour, they were packed and on their horses heading in a similar direction as the day before, where it was believed rain would fall that day.

Ella took comfort atop Chestnut, who twitched his ears happily when she stroked his thick, powerful neck. Her thighs had stopped protesting, growing accustomed to the long riding. She had made certain to pack dried lamb strips for later because she knew she'd need something before they broke for lunch.

The following hours were a repeat of the previous days and she feared it would all begin to blur and gain a sameness similar to *Groundhog Day*, although she could do without a rerun of the fight. She used the time to continue her observations, noting the sparseness of plant life that sustained the handful of animals and birds she saw. There was a paucity of snakes and lizards which surprised her, but she figured the desert was vast and the law of averages worked against her.

It was late in the day, another fruitless one spent searching for the elusive myth when the group encountered other nomads astride camels. It was a family—father, mother, and two children under twelve—with a fourth camel carrying their gear and looking none too pleased about it. Chenghiz waved then gestured for them to wait for them. The other family waved back and slowed, despite the still oppressive heat of the day.

"Sain baina uu," the man said as they neared.

"Sain baitsgaan uu," Chenghiz replied.

Names and greetings were exchanged, a practiced custom it seemed. The man was Delger, his wife Nomin, the son Ganzaya, and the daughter Üürtsaikh. There were pleasantries exchanged though most of Ella's team seemed impatient, ready to go back and have dinner and probably do more drinking. The prediction of rain proved inaccurate as the brief storm occurred to their west. To her, it was just a wasted day.

After they spoke in rapid Mongolian for a few minutes, with a lot of hand gestures, she studied the family, trying to imagine their lives. They moved at least twice a year, Jargal had told her. They tended sheep mostly, losing their grown children to the more attractive life in the cities. The children seemed healthy and content if in need of a bath. They shyly smiled at her, but their focus remained on the armed soldiers flanking the scientific team. No doubt seeing guns was a rarity for them. It was a lonely life for long stretches, but the only one they grew up knowing. Some, like Chenghiz and Jargal, turned from farming to focus on the growing tourist trade, often leading expeditions for private parties, competing with the established firms cashing in on interest in their "exotic" life.

Finally, there were waves and farewells, then the four moved on. As they receded from sight, Chenghiz and Jargal spoke in harsh whispers and she couldn't read their expressions but clearly, there was some disagreement. Some tones were universal.

"Delger said there was evidence of a worm a day ago," he said, his right hand gesturing in the direction they had come from, not far from the angle they had been a day before. So close, it seemed.

"What sort," Kozlov demanded.

"Tracks."

"No carcasses?"

Chenghiz shook his head.

"The desert isn't kind to the dead," Jargal added. "You got lucky. But he said there were long trails. Several, and they steered clear of the area, going hours out of their way. They know."

"That's not good enough," Lebedev snapped, the heat clearly getting the better of the older man. "I can't bring home sand."

"You may have nothing more to bring home than what you already have," Chenghiz warned. "I told you this at the outset."

Some of the soldiers snickered at the exchange, clearly finding the old man's sputter amusing. Ella felt for him, could sense the urgency Lebedev had brought to the project, and again she wondered why. This most definitely proved to be a frustrating trip. Would the evidence from day one be all they'd find? And what if the lab analysis showed it to be something other than Death Worm venom?

Her fears were made manifest over the course of the next few days. Each morning they rose, grumbled at the early hour, despite their guides and their assistants being up even earlier to prepare their breakfast. Everyone complained about the heat, mounted their horses, and rode for hours to find nothing. More bitching, moaning, and complaining, then they returned for dinner and varying amounts of drinking.

The only thing that differed between days two and eight were the rare occasions of crossing paths with other travelers. On day six, a pair of men told them that they too had seen the telltale wavy trail of the Death Worm, pointing in a direction a good forty-five degrees away from the one the family had indicated. If true, there was one well-traveled worm or several solitary ones. From what Jargal had told them, the worms never traveled in packs and that the worms laid their eggs and disappeared. How they were fertilized or how the baby Death Worms were nurtured no one ever said. That sent Ella into daydreams about plushy baby Death Worms as a souvenir item. However, if there were two or more in the area, that did increase the odds of them being located, something that energized the scientists.

What was clear, though, was that everyone they encountered was genuinely concerned about the Death Worm being active. She could sense their sincerity even if she didn't speak the language beyond the handful of words Chenghiz had taught her and most of those were directed at Chestnut.

Rodion had laughed at their fear, earning him scowls from Ella and the scientists. He was supposed to be on their side, believing in their prey so his actions were supportive, not derisive. Thankfully, it was a brief lapse. He had been behaving himself since the apology. They had managed to find times they could have some privacy, usually at night when the scientists were talking with the guides. He had come up behind her, pressing against her, and whispered, "Ne khochesh' perepikhnut'sya?" She nodded briefly and he took her by the hand, and they slipped into the ger and, under their blankets, they fumbled at their clothes, parting enough of them to make skin-to-skin contact. It was rough and quick and to a degree satisfying.

It was the best she felt. Most mornings, she was tired like the others, but there were days she never felt quite right, believing a combination of the unrelenting heat and salted foods were just not agreeing with her. The lamb was fine, but she needed more than that, knowing a life of fruits and vegetables was what she preferred. At those times, she kept telling herself "a few more days," a mantra to get her through the tough times.

Based on what they had learned on the sixth day, Lebedev got into an argument with his guides, insisting the entire ger camp be relocated closer to the sighting of worm trails, which apparently were clustered in a several-square mile area several hours away. He wanted to get closer, cutting down on the travel time, but Jargal wanted to be as far from the Death Worm as possible. It was resolved when he forked over a handful of brown 100 tögrög bills into her hand. She continued to complain but directed the two aides to be ready to break camp the following morning.

That allowed Ella to learn how one takes apart a ger, wrapping its walls around the contents, and strapping them to the camels. She appreciated doing something to break the monotony of riding a horse in the hot sun. This was productive, she could see the fruit of her labor, and the stretching was deemed good. Everyone pitched in to hurry things along, with Jargal directing the soldiers and scientists, sparing none of them from her critical judgment of their packing skills. Ella and Rodion found her amusing, the soldiers did not. Lebedev groused a bit about how late they were starting that day, but Jargal harshly reminded him this was being done at his behest.

The soldiers were even less thrilled to stand around, watching the two teen workers swiftly erect the framework of their ger when they arrived several hours southwest from their last position, almost due west at the edge of the desert border. The ground was hard, packed from the brief rains. Scrub brush had grown in the cracks and Ella finally managed to see some reptile life although she more fascinated by the small Gobi jerboa, its grayish and white fur, small forearms, and large eyes appealed to her. She learned in her research that it had been first identified a mere year before the Death Worm's first appearance in books. When the ger had been completed, she took her cell phone and carefully walked along the edge of a mountain to find a small group of the mammals. She snapped off several pictures and then took a video of them foraging for food. Now, this was the kind of fieldwork she preferred, observation and record-ing, as opposed to fruitlessly trekking through dry, mostly barren land.

Ella was in exceedingly good spirits when she walked back to the camp for dinner and Rodion took advantage of the mood, holding her in his arms, kissing her with ardor, not caring who could see them. The catcalls from some of the soldiers finally made them stop but she didn't feel embarrassed at all.

"You're all jealous, even you, Haajar!" he called. "You've never had lips this soft."

Haajar flipped him off and Ella giggled.

The night was spent in communal good humor, as everyone felt at least something productive had occurred, even if it was merely relocating the camp. There were songs and stories, laughter and goodwill. It was the best she had felt in days, so Ella easily drifted asleep.

So of course, that was when she heard an unnatural shrieking sound during the night. Everyone in the ger stirred, but the sol-diers rose faster and were already outside, flashlights scanning the grounds. Lebedev and Rodion emerged from the ger, but Fredek waved them back, to stay inside. The five soldiers fanned out, rifles and pistols at the ready. Chenghiz and one of the teens joined them, exploring the area.

It was the teen who made the discovery, crying out and summoning the soldiers. From the ger entrance, Ella could see them hurrying off, away from the camp and now her fear and cu-riosity were at war. The minutes ticked off and she heard sounds but, thankfully, no gunfire. The sounds were hard to make out, a mix of Mongolian and Russian, the tone unclear.

Finally, it was Valerik Belyaev who came to their ger and said, "Come, we've found something."

"Is it safe?" Lebedev asked.

"Now it is," the man said and turned to lead them to the others. Rodion made certain he walked protectively beside Ella, who shivered a bit in the cooler night air, even though it really wasn't cold enough. It was fear speaking throughout her body.

They walked perhaps a hundred yards from the camp, away from the embers that had been their campfire, the stars twinkling in the cloudless sky. If it hadn't been for the tension, it would have been a wonderful night of stargazing. Ella realized Jargal had hurried to catch up, ready to see matters that her husband tried to keep her from.

The cluster of people had formed a semicircle around the remains of a camel. One of the camp's animals, she recognized by its bridle. The animal must have gotten free and went wandering away. Something had seared away its pale brown hair and skin, exposing intestines, organs, and veins. A pool of blood and viscera pooling under it. The soldiers alternated between standing over the camel brandishing their guns and waving   flashlights and keeping their back to the dead beast, flashlights scanning the dark desert.

"Yebena mat," Rodion said, earning him a disapproving look from Lebedev, who now shone his own light on the camel.

"Look at the wound," Ella told him, her shivering increased.

"Bozhe moy," Lebedev and Kozlov murmured in unison as they spotted blotches of yellow, smoking against the corpse. Tiny wisps of steam floated straight up, caught in the crossing lights.

"Pictures," Smirnov snapped.

Rodion pulled out his cell phone and began taking pictures as others took video and still pictures from their own phones. Ella wondered why no one had a *real* camera at the moment. Ella forced herself closer to examine the wounds, confirming for herself that this matched the stories.

Lebedev stopped searching the distance and trained his flashlight on the camel. "Every angle, the scene, the camel, everything," he demanded.

The cameras clicked away, their flashes brighter than the lights the others held. As he worked, Grisha called out another discovery. Smirnov walked in his direction, careful to stay behind so as not to mar any further evidence. He joined the medic, and they stared in the distance, the cone of light showing a distinctive disruption of the ground. It was enough to have the scientist summon Rodion to come take more pictures.

"Everyone, stop moving," Lebedev commanded. It took a moment, but there was silence. "Now, do not step away from where you are. You *idioty* have already mucked up the scene. From where you stand, shine your lights out into the desert. Tell me what you see."

"You look for waves?" Timor asked.

"Da."

Eight lights fanned out, creating a circle radiating out into the dark, waving back and forth, searching for something that matched what had been seen before. As they did, Jargal murmured. The patterns and repetitions of her words reminded Ella of prayer. Maybe they'd need some divine help.

"Ella, my dear," Lebedev said quietly, "go and get the sample kit. We must have some of this acid, skin samples, organ samples, everything."

"Of course," she said and hurried off, noting with some comfort that Haajar shone her light to make certain Ella didn't feel alone. After all, if it really was the Death Worm, who knew where it was?

She hurriedly gathered the gear, remembering to bring extra gloves, and then returned. She was pleased when Kozlov allowed her to help take the samples, although he was like an overprotective father, making certain she didn't actually touch the yellowish acid that had killed the camel. While there, he took measurements, recording the information into a note app on his phone.

As she completed her work, she heard a male voice call out. Valerik, she would say, his tone high and excited, which caused a ripple of noise from the others. She forced herself to focus on her work, so she didn't burn herself. There was a certain thrill mixed in with the fear, excitement over doing the fieldwork she had imagined. Now they had two samples from different locations which would allow for better analysis. It would prove more conclusive and therefore worthwhile.

She held out her hand to help Lebedev rise to his feet and the two followed the others to where all the lights converged. It was not where Grisha had found the potential worm sign, it was further away and to the right.

"What is it?" the senior scientist asked.

Smirnov turned around, a look of surprise still on his features in the light and shadow. "A trail."

Ella and Lebedev joined him, and all three aiming their lights in the same direction, illuminating a thicker, wavier trail, but most definitely similar enough to be considered evidence of a Death Worm.

"Two?"

She looked at Lebedev, eyes wide. "Are you serious?"

"We can compare the images later, but to these tired eyes, the trails are sized differently. That suggests two Death Worms in the same vicinity."

She looked over her shoulder to see just how close their camp was to where not one, but two possible Mongolian Death Worms made mischief.

CHAPTER SIX

Timor Yegorov insisted his people work through the night, taking shifts walking the perimeter of the camp while everyone else tried to get some sleep. It was more a joke than anything else because no one felt like sleeping considering what they'd witnessed. Chenghiz passed around fresh fermented milk to help everyone sleep, but Ella refused, the smell making her unsettled. She sat on her bedding, arms wrapped around her knees, trying to imagine what would happen next. There was no leaving overnight, there was no idea when the Death Worm's optimal time of day to eat was. Or lay eggs. She or one of the others would have to go back for a more thorough examination to determine if the creature laid eggs. What a find that would be!

Rodion insisted on being a part of the patrol, to help the others, but the soldiers refused to give him a firearm, rendering him fairly useless. So, he returned to the ger, somewhat angry, somewhat relieved, and sipped at the drink.

"Didn't I promise you an adventure?"

Ella chuckled at that. "I never said you were a liar."

"Good. I do not lie when I can help it."

"And when can't you help but lie?"

"Usually when my boss asks something stupid, or a woman asks my opinion about her outfit."

She laughed at that and leaned into him, his arms wrapping protectively around her. They sat in silence for a long while.

"What do you think?"

"I think something's out there, dushka. I think it is deadly and dangerous and we are fortunate to have so many soldiers."

"Don't you think sending so many seemed excessive?"

"Maybe. Not now, of course. Now, I want a battalion." She nodded at that.

Finally, the adrenaline wore off and exhaustion dragged her down until she nodded off, her head on Rodion's shoulder, his arms cradling her.

The loud repeat of gunfire startled them both. The first thing Ella noted was the dim arrival of the sun, realizing she did get a few hours' rest. Her heart thumped as she scrambled to her feet with Rodion, who stifled a yawn. The three scientists were also alert, sitting up on their bedding. Rodion rushed to the door and peered out as a third shot resounded. Valerik rushed by, rifle in hand, warning them to stay inside. Still, both peered through the doorway in the direction of the gunshot, which was not where the camel had been attacked.

A few minutes passed without another shot or much sound at all. Finally, Timor walked into sight and gave everyone the thumbs up.

"What the hell?" Rodion asked.

"Fredek saw something move in the dim light and fired. Either he missed or there was nothing to hit."

"But is there a trail?"

"Da."

With that, Rodion grabbed the camera and rushed out in the direction of the other soldiers. He snapped a series of pictures, including closeups of the wavy ground where two bullets pocked the ground. Ella joined him and recorded measurements on her cell phone. This and the one from earlier were nearly identical. More evidence of something. When she gave the measurements to Lebedev and Smirnov, they were delighted, but also concerned that at least one of the creatures was still nearby.

As they murmured among themselves, Ella noted Chenghiz close enough to overhear the conversation. Their eyes met, hers questioning and his staring ahead, uncertainty clear in his gaze.

He appeared rattled, his disbelief now openly being challenged, which seemed to bother him. Ella felt an icy chill skitter down her spine. *Something* was out there, and it was deadly.

Skipping breakfast, Ella joined Rodion as they downloaded the pictures to the sole laptop they had brought along. They went picture by picture, enlarging several to take a closer look. In time, they were joined by Kozlov and Lebedev, who studied the measurements. There was no excursion that day. It was time to research and plan, then make informed decisions as to what to do next.

Ella was glad science led the expedition but was worried about what would happen should the worm or worms reappear. Could bullets harm it? Just how far did the acid fly? And what about the reported electrical discharges? What had seemed myth a week ago now felt all too real. And all too dangerous.

CHAPTER SEVEN

Lebedev, Smirnov, Kozlov, Rodion, and Ella worked through the morning to compile preliminary findings. There were most definitely gaps in their research findings and they lacked a proper lab to study the specimens collected. More than once, the elder scientist cursed not having a plane or helicopter at his disposal to rush things back to Mongolia or Russia for further study. He did use the satellite phone to reserve lab space for his return and then made some other calls, although Ella had no idea to whom since he walked away from them.

The soldiers continued to patrol the area, stifling yawns, allowing one at a time to nap. Jargal comforted the teen who believed himself responsible for improperly securing the camel so it got loose and wound up a victim. His high-pitched wails grated, but Ella couldn't blame him for his grief and guilt. Jargal proved very motherly to the boy. The softening of her hard demeanor surprised Ella.

Finally, Jargal put the boy to work making lunch then went off to study the camel, wanting to see if the saddle and bridle were salvageable. After all, the tack cost them money, which was always an issue.

Rodion wanted to see the camel in daylight and Ella felt compelled to come along, which he objected to. She shot him a look that immediately caused him to back down, hands of surrender in the air. Haajar insisted she come along to watch the surroundings as they focused on the corpse. It was already a smelly affair, the sun baking the insides, insects settling in for an unexpected feast. Rodion brought along his magnifying glass while Ella carried the camera just in case. After catching one strong whiff from the beast, she gagged, then vomited, wrapping a handkerchief around her lower face to help filter the stench. In the end, it didn't do much good but psychologically, it helped.

"Anything?" she asked.

"No sign of eggs. Just rotting meat."

"Do they eat camel?"

"It is not a Mongolian staple, no. It is popular elsewhere, usually African countries," he told her.

Ella and Haajar exchanged bemused glances and then she turned to Robion, her face mock serious. "So, you're not just a pretty face?" she teased, trying to lighten the mood.

"I am so much more than just a pretty face."

Haajar groaned audibly at that, rolling her eyes at Ella, who laughed. "Idiot, she was asking if the Death Worm ate camel."

Rodion shot Ella a look and she shrugged, letting him twist at the gibe.

"Well, genius, do they?" the soldier asked.

"We do not know what they eat," Rodion told her.

"So, the answer is, you don't know. Just great. You're all going to get us killed."

A somber group gathered for lunch and Lebedev led a briefing for the group, summarizing what they knew. For a change, the soldiers were unusually attentive to scientific detail. The situation was now edging toward their area of expertise. Everyone ate slowly and silently as Ella hoped the gruesome topic wouldn't spoil her meal. It was the first time she had felt truly hungry in days.

"A detailed analysis, well, as best we could make with the tools available, strongly suggests that there are not one but two Death Worms in the vicinity."

"We haven't seen it, or them, so we don't know what it is," Chenghiz challenged.

Lebedev frowned at that but conceded the point. "All evidence to date matches the oral testimony as to how the Mongolian Death

Worm operates. It burrows underground and travels close to the surface. It emerges to strike its victim. In this case the camel, in the other case an ass. In both cases, there is a yellowish residue left behind, which correlates with the anecdotal evidence that the creature secretes a deadly toxin or perhaps acid, which burns through the skin with remarkable speed, quickly killing the victim."

"How do you know it is quick?" Chenghiz asked, enjoying playing devil's advocate.

"We all heard the poor animal's scream last night. By the time any of us arrived, it was already dead, its attacker gone from sight. That suggests speed on the part of the secretion and the killer."

The Mongolian nodded in approval.

"What is that? Venom? Acid? Something else?" Timor asked.

"I wish I knew," Lebedev said. "It acts like an acid, but the beast was dead. The acid burned through the skin and affected the major organs, but it should have been writhing in agony for some time, not dead so quickly."

"No residue to analyze?" Haajar asked.

"Not enough and we don't have the right equipment for a proper analysis," Lebedev admitted.

"It was a mercy," Jargal said.

There were nods of approval all around.

"All of this fits the profile of the Death Worm, but we still have no evidence of the creature itself."

"You really think there are two?" Grisha asked.

"I do and here is why. We have photographic evidence of two different wavy indentations in the ground, in two very different locations, and one is wider than the other by more than a few centimeters.

"Are there any stories of them traveling in pairs or packs?" Ella asked.

"None," Jargal said. "All the stories we know are about one worm."

"But you say they lay eggs, so that says there's definitely more than one worm out there," she added.

"We don't have enough hard data to know how it operates. Just how it moves and how it kills."

"Were there any eggs in the camel?" Timor asked.

"None," Rodion confirmed. When Lebedev cast a questioning glance, Rodion explained the mid-morning examination, receiving a satisfied nod.

"Are we compromised?" Timor asked.

"I said we shouldn't have moved," Jargal interjected. The woman could have quit but chose not to. Clearly, there was a part of her that wanted this matter settled, no matter how she complained.

"I wish I could say with some confidence that we're fine because the Death Worm has struck here and there is no evidence or testimony suggesting it revisits a spot," Lebedev said. "However, we are in an unprecedented situation. No one has ever reported encountering two in one area, so we cannot know why this is happening and therefore whether or not we are in danger."

"Then, from an operational standpoint, we should relocate again, probably miles away to be safe. How far do these things go?" Timor asked.

One of the teens groaned at the prospect of breaking down and rebuilding the camp a second time, earning him a harsh look from Chenghiz, whose bronze face shone with sweat.

"We need to stay nearby to observe, in case they come back or more arrive," Lebedev argued. "This is our chance to catch one, which is the primary point of the expedition."

Timor didn't look happy but recognized that he was there to serve the professor, who was authorized by the government he'd sworn his allegiance to. Ella to wondered why they wanted a live worm. Why now when they've had that carcass since 1972?

In the end, they decided to remain in place and not venture far from the campground. As the sun set, two rotating guards would patrol. Tomorrow, their penultimate day of the expedition, Lebedev would determine what should be done next. No one even broached the notion of extending the trip. He resumed working on the laptop with Kozlov, leaving Smirnov, Ella, and

Rodion free. The scientist suggested they revisit the two trails and see what they could learn. Ella made sure Timor knew and asked Grisha to accompany them. She would have preferred someone else, in case Rodion reacted badly again, but no one else was free.

They walked slowly, the heat radiating from the ground and the sky. Ella was thankful they were near the camp so she could have water and a nap when they were done. Being so tired had become old, but she pushed ahead, telling herself just two days to go.

"Do you think Lebedev will get an extension if he thinks we're close?" she asked.

"Who can say?" Smirnov said.

"I hope not," Grisha added, and they all nodded in agreement. No one wanted to stay in the heat or be at risk.

The camel remained in place, no longer steaming but still slowly baking in the heat. The decomposition would be quick, but the smell was horrific. After making one circuit to see that nothing had changed, they headed for the first trail. Grisha bent low to look at it closely.

"It has to be at least seventeen centimeters wide," he estimated.

"So, seventeen centimeters by a meter and a half long," Rodion said. "Approximately."

"I wonder what it weights," Ella said.

"It has a skeletal structure, but probably something lightweight," Rodion theorized. Digestive organs, reproductive organs, heart, lungs, venom sacs... maybe eight kilograms?"

"At least. From the drawings and stories, I would think maybe heavier. Ten?"

"Could be."

"I concur," Smirnov said approvingly.

They studied the exit point but found nothing but dirt, nothing to suggest how the worm moved. Rodion then walked the length of the wavy trail, using a measuring tape to take readings. It was over three meters long and then vanished, so it had come up to the near-surface and tracked its prey. That proved to be a fascinating aspect to Ella, one no one had considered previously.

"Could we dig here," she asked, indicating the terminus, "and see how far down it went?"

"While we do have shovels, if it's still down there, I wouldn't want to be the one to disturb it," Smirnov said.

"If only we had lidar," she mused.

"An expensive toy for our expedition," Smirnov said. "And, I admit, one we didn't anticipate needing."

The quartet then silently walked to where the other trail was found. They took more measurements and discovered this one was just over three meters long, but it lacked an exit. Whatever it had been heading for moved or got distracted.

"I wonder if the gunfire scared it off," Grisha mused, practicing his English.

"Could be," Ella agreed.

"Whatever happened, it didn't emerge. And it is significantly wider so definitely a second worm," Smirnov said.

"Do you think these will come back tonight?"

"We don't even know why it emerged last night," Rodion said. "True. There's zero evidence of the worm consuming any part of the camel," Smirnov said.

"And no eggs," Ella added. "Hey, so exactly what do the Death Worms eat allowing them to hibernate ten months of the year?"

Both Smirnov and Rodion shrugged.

"So, more questions than answers," Rodion said, somewhat deflated.

The four explorers continued to wander the vicinity, seeking out a possible trail but after half an hour of seemingly walking in circles, Smirnov declared there was nothing left to discover so they all returned to the camp. As they walked, Ella noted for the first time there was a cluster of gray clouds in view, seemingly headed their way. She gestured for the others to see them and there was some surprise.

"That wasn't on the map," Smirnov said.

"Rain might coax them out, right?" Grisha asked.

Ella wasn't sure if that was what she really wanted or not. Sure, finding and capturing one would be a great scientific and cultural find, but she wasn't sure that even with five soldiers they could contain a creature the size they estimated. And then, exactly what would they do with it? Removing the specimen from its natural habitat could kill it, or at very least skew the test results. But still, that was why they were here.

By the time they returned to camp, there was a sense of excitement in the air as others had noticed the clouds and the prospect of rain. Lebedev had already had the large plastic containers they brought along were inspected and placed outside the ger for rapid use. The teens hurried about, securing things that might be ruined in the rain, already Under Jargal's supervision, they delivered provisions to each ger. Setting the foodstuffs in the kitchen, they suggested it would be best to cook their own dinner in place.

"What do you think," Smirnov asked Lebedev when they were reunited.

"There wasn't supposed to be a storm today, so who can say?"

Standing nearby, Chenghiz said, "It happens. Look at how dark they are. They're carrying a lot of water, and it's already starting out there." He gestured and everyone looked to see the curtain of gray that connected the clouds to the ground.

"How long before it gets here?" Kozlov asked.

"An hour, if we're lucky. Don't ask for how long, I am a guide, not a weatherman."

With the gear under tarps or inside a ger, everything was secure. Timor considered keeping a watch outside, even in the rain, but after consulting with Lebedev, it was decided everyone would hunker down. The rains weren't likely to last long and there had never been a story about the Death Worm attacking a campsite. Of course, there hadn't been stories of two trails either, so everything was really an unknown.

Inside their ger, the scientists and interns played cards for a few hours, tallying up fictional debts that it had been made clear to Ella, would never be collected. It was a passable enough time as the first patter of rain hit their roof and drips fell from the opening at the top. It had been decided that any cooking could wait, so they nibbled on stale bread, some cheese, and dried meat as the rains arrived and settled over the campsite for a while. It proved to be a light, steady rain, the ground absorbing the moisture fast enough that no one worried about their ger getting soaked. The woolen wall coverings proved remarkably effective at keeping dry, impressing Ella. The hole at the top let in some rain, which harmlessly pattered against the stove.

When everyone had grown tired of cards, they tried to make a fire that would not be extinguished by the rain. The burning dung and wood scraps that fueled it, stank up the confined space, spoiling whatever appetite Ella had. Knowing the older men as she did, she suspected she was expected to fulfill the traditional role of woman cooking for the men. To undermine that to a degree, she insisted Rodion come help her prepare. He did so without complaint, which pleased her. He proved to be a passable sous chef as she prepared a broth for the meat, adding crumbled cheese, to provide something warm, tasty, and frankly, different from what had been served previously. She had wished for more seasonings and definitely some vegetables but those were at least than forty-eight hours away.

The rain continued as they ate, their conversation inconsequential, everyone having grown tired of talking almost exclusively about the Death Worm. Unfortunately, that turned to their mutual affection for bandy, which she took to understand was their form of ice hockey with far less physical contact than the North American version she was more familiar with. Apparently, Kozlov and Lebedev had a long-running competition in something called Russian Pyramid, which she gathered was a cue and balls game with fifteen balls, and the cue ball was red, of course.

"When we go home, I will teach it to you," Kozlov said.

Rodion instinctively leaned into her and said, "Nyet, I will teach it to my dushka." She rolled her eyes and Kozlov laughed.

"Ah to be young and in love," he said.

"My young bride here will make me very happy," Rodion said.

They toasted the couple, but Ella was conflicted. Each time he used "bride" it caused her to wince. She was not interested in getting married or the presumption of the children that would follow. Not now. Not with Rodion. She had grad school and her career ahead of her. Only once she had established herself professionally would she consider getting married. And if she was traveling, children would only complicate things She had always been on the fence about being a mother and now, at twenty-three, was certainly not the time to be making any decisions.

Of course, she felt something for Rodion and knew he was being affectionate with the term but could she picture a life with him? Surely he would insist on staying in Russia. Could she stand to be so far from her family and friends? Was there even a place for her there in academia, and would she have the freedom to do the fieldwork she had imagined for herself? It was certainly nothing they had discussed. It was clear he lived in the moment while she thought in longer terms, which was just one of their many differences. She just didn't know, and there would be less than two months when they returned for her to make up her mind.

The rain continued and there was nothing left to do but sleep. They prepared for an early night. As they did, in a now-familiar communal style, Lebedev was asked what the plan was for their final day.

"The rains might coax it… *them* out. We'll see the conditions in the morning. If nothing presents itself, we'll see what Chenghiz suggests."

"He's not buying this yet, is he?" Smirnov said.

"He was a skeptic a week ago, now he's less certain, that's for sure," Lebedev said with a short laugh.

"What about you, Ella, have you come to believe in the worm?" Smirnov asked. "As I recall, you had some doubts."

She had to be careful with her answer since they'd be writing up an evaluation of her performance. The actual tasks were performed with satisfaction, but she kept asking questions no one could answer. Ella realized she needed their goodwill to ensure she received full credit for this three-month stint, otherwise, she would have wasted time and someone's money. "I don't doubt something killed those animals, but the Mongolian Death Worm has too many unanswered questions."

"What do *you* think did all this?" Lebedev said.

"Nothing I've ever researched. Something new," she said before adding, "and that's what makes this so fascinating."

"Fascinating," Lebedev repeated as if tasting the word. "I like that. Fascinating."

Inwardly, she exhaled.

Soon, the lights were extinguished and everyone's breathing evened out as one by one, they fell asleep. Everyone except Ella, who found she couldn't sleep. She tossed and turned, unable to get comfortable, her mind switching between thoughts of the creature and thoughts of Rodion and the future. At that moment, the unknown future scared her more than the unknown creature out there, somewhere. She tried to imagine what life for her would be like in Russia, certain she couldn't coax the proud Russian to join her in America. Her thoughts tumbled back and forth as she adjusted herself, with sleep remaining just beyond her reach.

There was a sound of someone moving, nearby enough for her to realize it was Rodion. For a brief moment, she thought he would come to her, and they could have some quiet pleasure, but no, he moving toward the wooden door. She had no idea how late it was, or how long she'd been lying there awake, but he seemed to be heading out to relieve himself, despite the rain.

He was gone for a minute or more before she heard the scream. It was a human cry of incredible pain, ululating and rising in both pitch and volume. She had no weapon and had no idea if the soldiers ever stationed a night guard. The screams continued then she heard a gurgling of some sort. Everyone went into motion at the same time, but she was closest to the door and flung it open, getting a face full of rain. She attempted to leave but Kozlov grabbed her arm and pulled her back inside.

They heard the rain on the ground, but nothing else.

Across the camp, three of the soldiers — Haajar, Valerik, and, thankfully, Grisha — tumbled out of their ger, the medic holding a lantern, the other two with rifles upraised. None had bothered with rain gear, reacting to the sound with urgency. They hurried toward where the shriek had sounded. As they moved out of sight, Ella slumped down, her tears mixing with the rain. That sound had been human... and that meant that, as the camel the night before, Rodion was dead.

Her stomach dropped; a well-spring of emotion flooded her. Not that long ago she considered how she felt for him and whether or not their relationship had a chance. Her heart was torn, but her brain said no. And even so, this sudden loss, the inability to bring closure of some sort to the relationship... it felt like something had been taken from her. A growing ember of anger joined her grief. Whatever took her lover's life needed to pay for this, but how could she fight something unseen? Something that could easily kill human or animal? It didn't matter to her, all that mattered was that the creature had to die.

Ella froze, paralyzed with emotional pain. Standing in the doorframe, the rain soaked through her shirt and shorts, plastering both to her skin. She was dimly aware of shouts and movement, but she couldn't focus. The ger was now empty and she heard footsteps wetly slapping along the ground. Lights waved, illuminating the pattering rainfall, but she couldn't focus on them, had no idea where everyone was. Well, that wasn't true. She knew Rodion had left the ger to pee, had died fulfilling a biological function, and his body lying in the dark just beyond the campsite. Idly, her scientific mind wondered about the acid, how it might react with human skin and tissue, possibly diluted from the rain, which might have prolonged his agony, the speed with which it killed him, which led her to consider they'd want to autopsy him but wait, there was no equipment to do a proper autopsy or a cooling chest to place the body until they could return to Ulaanbaatar, and who would have to tell his parents, parents she never met but only heard about in stories, Rodion certain she'd love them and they love her, but now that meeting would happen at the funeral where they would likely blame her for his being a part of the expedition even though it was their son, their now-dead son, who invited her along so the blame really needed to be placed on her mentor... who was... who was....

Her body shook with heaving sobs, slumping to the ground as the rain fell and she sat alone in the doorway.

Finally, Kozlov filled her vision. He crouched beside her, resting on his heels, and handed her a towel. She took it with a shaking hand and wiped her face. At some point, the rain let up, and then suddenly stopped. It was still night. Noises filled the darkness, people rushed around but no shots had been fired, no one else screamed.

The professor remained where he was, quietly offering companionship until she was ready to rise.

"He's gone."

He nodded at her, and she cried some more, sniffed, dabbed at her face, and took a deep breath. Kozlov helped her up and they stood with her uncertain what to do. Should she join the others on the hunt, despite a part of her mind saying the killer would not be found? Should she, could she, see the body?

"Stay here," he said as if reading her mind.

Haajar and Lebedev came into sight and walked slowly over to them. The older man looked sad and weary, placing a hand on her shoulder. They exchanged no words, their looks conveying silent messages. Even the female soldier looked sadder than anything else and there was a sympathetic look when their eyes met.

"What now," she finally asked.

"It's nearly midnight," Lebedev said. "We can't go anywhere until the morning. We'll pack and go back early."

She nodded.

"We'll be patrolling until dawn," Hajar assured her and then walked off, back toward the others, back to where Rodion's body lay cooling.

"You should try and sleep," Kozlov said.

"Not likely," she replied, her voice surprising her in how rough it sounded.

"Then rest."

"Not likely."

With that, the two men entered the ger, uncertain what else to done. Slowly, the others began to drift back into the camp. First were the two teens, taut with fright, with Jargal shooing them from behind, her voice encouraging, her face a mask. Then came Smirnov, his face grief-stricken. He also placed a comforting hand on her shoulder as he passed her.

"Rodion did good work," was all he could manage. It was quite likely that none had experienced loss on a field trip before and were uncertain how to process it for themselves or how to offer his girlfriend any comfort.

The soldiers filed past, most giving her looks but none daring to come close. Grisha wasn't with them, presumably still with the body or on patrol.

The last was Chenghiz, who walked directly to her, cupped her face in his rough hands, and solemnly kissed both cheeks. "The distance between heaven and earth is no greater than one thought," he softly said. "He shouldn't have died, but his memory remains."

"Another proverb?"

He nodded in agreement.

"Thank you," she said quietly.

Unlike the others, he lingered by her in companionable silence.

Finally, she asked, "What can we do for him?"

"Dr. Lebedev wants to do a closer examination in the morning," he replied.

"I suppose he needs to," she said.

"Yes, even here we have paperwork. We will need to file reports and with pictures. I don't know how to explain the yellow stains or the way he died."

His voice was low, matter-of-fact matter not devoid of emotion. He clearly felt the loss as a man, not as a guide responsible for the group, or the possible loss of business or even a possible lawsuit, things that might preoccupy people in Russia or America. No, this was a man mourning another man.

"How do you bury your dead?" she asked.

"A family member is supposed to remove the things that might make his spirit want to remain on earth. Something he might want with him in death. Whatever it is, it's located and disposed of so when the soul is reincarnated bad luck does not follow him."

She had forgotten that being a majority Buddhist people, they believed in reincarnation, and she idly thought about what he might want to come back as or did the soul not have a say? She didn't know.

"And then?"

"If he died in the ger, he'd be removed through a hole in the wall, not the doorway to prevent evil spirits from following. But he died outdoors and that would give him a sky burial. The body is left outdoors after the ceremony, led by a local lama, somewhere high, in an unprotected place so he is exposed to the elements. The soul is gone, the body an empty vessel to return to the earth."

"Where would you find a lama?"

"Jargal knows of several and we'd send word with the boys. It would take a day or more."

"But they want to leave in the morning. Do we bring him back to Ulaanbaatar with us?"

Chenghiz shook his head. "I suppose so, but it feels wrong."

She shuddered at the idea of traveling back to the city with the body nearby. The idea of leaving him here, to be picked apart by birds and reptiles wasn't appealing either. She thought of his parents and knew they'd want him home, for them to bury according to their customs.

"I think it has to be done that way," she said.

"I know."

They remained in silence for a time until he let out a loud breath and moved. "I am going to make sure everything is secure; everyone is in bed and try to get some rest. You should, too."

Before he moved, she threw her arms around him and hugged him tightly. He didn't seem to know how to react, and she suspected she broke some taboo but didn't really care. She needed it.

She entered the ger and was surprised the three men were sleeping or pretending to sleep. Ella changed into dry clothes and then sat on the bedding and couldn't imagine trying to sleep. Not now and maybe not for a long time. She ached, she felt empty, and she noted the spark of anger near her heart had yet to dissipate. After trying to relax and finding it impossible, she rose quietly and left the ger taking comfort in knowing there was someone else out there.

It was eerily quiet outside. The ground having sucked in the moisture, was already drying out in the arid night air. There was a quarter moon and brilliant stars, but she paid them scarce attention. Instead, she began walking and realized her feet were taking her toward Rodion. Grisha was out there, somewhere on patrol, probably walking the perimeter. While he was a nice guy, she didn't want to see anyone else right now. She wanted to cloak herself in grief and just walk.

The path was clear and the light from the campfire faded behind her as she left the campsite and entered the desert. The wide pattern of depressions suggested all the feet that had rushed back and forth since Rodion was killed. And now she was leaving her own imprint, her way of paying homage to the man she might have loved. As she walked, shapes came into view. Apparently, Rodion had peed and walked toward the camel carcass that lay in that direction or had gone further out than necessary to complete his business.

Something glistening caught her eye, but it was not near Rodion's body, which was thankfully just a dark silhouette. No, this was something angled toward the camel. She sniffed and something acrid was in the air, something she had noted previously but could not identify. It wasn't coming from the camel but from the dampness on the ground. At that moment, she wished for both a gun and a flashlight. Goosebumps sprung to attention on her arms and her breathing got heavier. Whatever left this residue—she stopped herself. She knew exactly what left this residue. It was the killer. The Death Worm. Like a movie criminal, it returned to the scene of the crime. Had it come to feed, did they kill and wait a day for the acid to complete its work? That was an interesting notion, something for the scientist within her to contemplate tomorrow. Right now, she was, she supposed, hunting.

The Death Worm hadn't come to eat. There'd been no real evidence it consumed its prey. It was not something raised in any of the oral histories. She finally remembered through her emotional haze that the Death Worm was said to lay its eggs in the victim and last night, she'd been disturbed. Two worm trails… One female followed by one male, searching to fertilize the eggs? One hypothesis, anyway.

Ella removed her cell phone from a pocket, thumbed the flashlight on, and neared the dead camel, which seemed misshapen—maybe bloated from internal gases building up? There was also a different scent in the air, something tangy and sickening at the same time. Then she heard a moist sound, something maybe sucking, but an active noise so she was instantly alert, now wishing Grisha and his rifle were closer. Still, she couldn't help herself, nearing the camel to see what was making the sound.

Carefully, she took one small step after another, inching and angling herself trying to get a better view. The harsh light didn't cast a cone of visible ground nearly large enough to calm her nerves.

The loose sand shifted beneath her feet. She stumbled forward a few jarring steps, just managing to stay upright, her light arcing into the night sky. As she righted herself, a blur of motion burst from the remains of the acid-burned hole in the camel's abdomen! She fumbled for a moment then activated the camera's video recorder. The thing was a dull red, and her clinical mind noted that the spiky protrusions she'd been told about were missing from the front. Instead, the flat front was round and seemed pinched close. There were no discernable eyes, ears, or nostrils as she had heard, but something alerted it to her presence. It writhed with startling speed, seemingly hurling itself out of the camel and toward her. As the creature cleared the camel, Ella took note of the small wet, round pebbles... its, no *her* eggs, still damp from being emitted from her cloaca.

Ella backpedaled, stumbling at first, then hurrying backward, refusing to take her eyes off the creature. It was segmented, she saw, remarkably flexible and was maneuvering directly toward her so she had to have some sensory apparatus that was undefined. Part of her emotional mind scolded the clinical part of her mind to focus on getting away alive and think about details later. She picked up speed, but to her surprise, the Death Worm was now speeding up, closing the gap between them.

The first several segments reared up, and the pinched mouth sprouted, a deadly flower now in bloom. A thin, steady stream of yellow acid arced from the opening, curving through the air. Thankfully, it landed short, missing Ella's right foot by inches. Startled, she dropped her cell phone, its flash aimed away from the creature.

It was time to turn on the afterburners. She drew ahead, the worm in pursuit, but thankfully, not gaining any ground.

She stole glances over her shoulder, first zigging right, then zagging left, but she was moving away from the camp and further into the desert, the cell phone's light even dimmer the further she moved from the gers. With one misstep, she felt a sharp pain in her ankle, and her gait changed. Every step that followed now agonizing. She wanted to cry out, but now she could make no sound. That was when she realized she was crying and her throat filling with phlegm. She was incapable of summoning help, so she continued to go one way, then another, the eerily quiet worm adjusting but losing ground. She presumed the somewhat tacky ground from the rain was helping slow it down.

She kept moving but couldn't notice everything, which is when her heel slipped over a stone, and she spiraled backward, landing hard on her butt. With her momentum stopped and sprawled in place, the Death Worm was coming right for her.

CHAPTER EIGHT

Ella swallowed hard then let out a cry for help at the top of her lungs. She was afraid the vast expanse of the desert would swallow her words. The Death Worm writhed across the ground, coming within range of another acid spray. There was no knowing how much acid she carried or how quickly she manufactured the weapon. All Ella knew was that if the worm touched her, she'd burn, and if the acid landed in the wrong place, there'd be two bodies to take back to Russia. Her parents barely understood what she was doing in the Gobi Desert looking for a worm when her specialty was mammals. How would the officials explain it, how would they justify bringing an American student on a potentially dangerous trip to another country?

She scrambled to her feet. Her right ankle throbbed the more weight she put on it. With a twist of her torso, Ella aimed her cries toward the campsite as she continued to limp at her best speed, hoping Grisha or someone else would hear her. The worm trailed perhaps fifteen feet behind her — and was gaining.

There was a sound to her left, something breaking, then she heard a rumble followed by an explosion of dirt and stone. The second Death Worm had decided to join the party and for the briefest of moments, Ella contemplated if there was some manner in which the two were in communication. It was more likely the second — perhaps the male — was in the vicinity, somehow involved in the eggs. Most fertilization occurred internally prior to the eggs being laid, but who knew how Mongolian Death Worms worked?

The second worm emerged, wider, longer, and a brighter red, its maw already open, ready to spray. Adrenaline surged, and she focused entirely on speed and distance as now there were two pursuers. She forced herself to ignore the pain and deal with the leg damage later; now was the time to *move*. Were they after her because she represented a threat to the eggs, or she was alive, and they were hungry, or they attacked anything that moved? She wished she could merely observe them going for their prey, not *being* the prey.

Welcome shouts sounded behind her, drawing closer, but she couldn't tell how far off as she moved further away from her dropped phone. She continued to evade, praying the soldiers reached her soon. Every step sent jagged shards of pain up her leg, but she'd worry about lasting damage later, once she survived.

Pounding footsteps approached, followed by a male cry, "Get out of the way!"

Ella pivoted to her right and cut a different angle, opening up a clear path to the two beasts. Rifle fire shattered the night, multiple shots almost in unison. They all missed the worms, but it did cause the pair to pause, reacting to something, probably the sound. For all she knew, they smelled the gunpowder.

There was a second volley, some of the bullets digging into the dirt between her and the worms, which determined the guns weren't a threat (she hoped they were wrong), and resumed pursuing her. Ella kept in motion, still zig-zagging the best she could, now limping badly.

The soldiers had fanned out, coming at the worms from several angles. It was five against two, but who knew if their skin was impervious to bullets or how many it would take to seriously wound them.

Valerik Belyaev was there, at her side, and he knelt to take aim directly at one of the worms. He steadied himself and then squeezed the trigger. The loud report hurt her ears, momentarily deafening and distracting her. The next thing she knew, the soldier beside her screamed as the acid spray washed over him.

His hands released the AK-47, stray acid scoring the metal and wooden stock. It tumbled to the ground as he screamed, the acid eating through his fingers and uniform shirt.

The other four soldiers focused their attention on the larger of the two worms and their concentrated fire seemed to do the trick. It made a sound, a definite shriek of pain in some high-pitched noise that came from deep within the beast. The segmented skin shredded and it rose, trying to twist and turn away, only to collapse as more lead plowed into its body. It jerked and spasmed, acid spraying uselessly, the spiked tail waving and making contact only with air.

It then stopped moving and seemingly deflated to the ground.

But as they focused on the larger threat and Ella watching, the other had come closer to her. She tried to rise and move, but her injured ankle refused to cooperate. As the worm drew closer and closer, Ella fumbled for the fallen rifle. Her fingers burned as she touched an acid-coated spot. She whipped her hand away, wiping it on the dirt to get the acid off her before it caused serious damage.

The second worm undulated closer, not opening its maw.

Ella silently prayed to God and her parents, begging for forgiveness.

The worm paused less than a foot from her. If it had eyes, Ella would have said it was studying her, but it held its position for one heartbeat, then two, then three. After six, it seemed to sprout a ring of something from its segmented sections — maybe tendrils, maybe tiny claws. Whatever it was, they worked fast, digging into the ground. Within seconds, its head sank beneath the surface, and dirt was thrown out of the tunnel.

One of the soldiers spotted this, gave a cry, and fired, missing the back half of the creature. Several more shots followed, at least one or two making contact, although they hardly seemed to slow the worm down. It continued to dig, with less and less of it visible.

Ella dared not touch it, in case its skin was as deadly as legend held. Her fingers were already sore, burning.

"Grisha!" she yelled.

The handsome medic arrived, looking at her damaged fingers while the other three protected them as the last of the worm vanished from sight.

"What did we just see?" Timor asked, still breathing hard from the last few minutes.

"Mongolian Death Worms," Ella said with conviction.

"So, they're real," Haajar said.

"Ask Valerik," Grisha said grimly.

"And Rodion," Ella added.

CHAPTER NINE

With the firing over, Chenghiz came out of the campground to assess the situation before anyone else could leave the area. He carried a pistol, some old model he had kept under wraps the entire week, and a flashlight, moving warily toward the cluster of people.

"öö khairt ezen mini," he said quietly as he saw the body of the dead soldier.

Timor gave him a quick rundown of the situation.

"Well, Dr, Lebedev will be happy to at least have a fresh sample," the guide said. He made certain Ella was going to be fine, as Grisha first wrapped her damaged fingers, then her ankle. The tightness of the ace bandage comforted her. She gave him a weak smile as he left, walking over to see the worm corpse for himself.

Ella heard him mumbling in Mongolian, suspecting there were prayers involved. With two dead and the Death Worm proved a reality, he had much to pray about. She hoped it brought him some comfort. She and religion hadn't been on speaking terms the last few years but now might be a good time to reconsider that stance.

Her mind was awhirl, but slowly the scientist in her rose up and demanded attention. She thought over the last hour and realized how much happened in such a short time. They not only had a specimen to bring back for study but there was more: the eggs. She had to get the scientists out here to gather them from the camel before other lifeforms found them. Who knew what happened to the eggs after they were laid? More than that, no one knew their gestation period, which she suspected must be short, with their hibernation period beginning in a few weeks, or really long, the ten months before the rainy season began again. Either way, the eggs had to be studied in a safe environment.

Rodion and Valerik paid a heavy price to obtain them.

Grisha and Fredek helped her hobble back to the camp as Haajar and Timor kept watch, in case the second, live worm, decided to come back. No one knew if they were intelligent enough to seek revenge or would sense more prey. So many questions.

As she neared the camp, the three scientists rushed toward Ella, Jargal keeping her distance, arms wrapped around herself. She had always believed but the reality had shaken her. Chenghiz followed right behind them and when the couple met, they embraced, tightly holding on to one another.

"My god, Ella, are you all right?" Lebedev asked.

"Not really," she said shakily. She shivered despite it not being particularly cold and could not stop herself. A part of her told her this was part of the shock, and she deserved this condition. It meant she was still alive.

Grisha quickly explained Ella's various injuries then hurried off to get her some water as the others, even Jargal, fussed over her. They offered so many apologies. Apologies for Rodion's death. Apologies for her injuries. Apologies for so much not going right.

She listened without reaction, huddled under a blanket Lebedev placed around her shoulders. Still, she shivered.

Grisha returned with a canteen, watching as she drank, then insisting she drink more. The good patient obeyed the order despite suddenly feeling nauseous from everything that had happened.

"Listen," she finally said, stopping the scientists from further babbling. It took a moment, but the overlapping voices fell silent, and she quickly recounted the news about not only a corpse but eggs. "My cell phone should have recorded the beasts in motion. Has anyone seen it?"

Head shook all around her, with several saying they'd look for it. The scientist's eyes brightened, several actual smiled. Someone dared to say "good work" as if she had anything to do with either specimen.

They were clearly eager to go see all this for themselves and personally gather the remains for transportation. Smirnov summoned over the two teens, who had been keeping out of the way, to come to assist them. He gave them orders and supervised as the other two went for Rodion's camera and more flashlights.

With all of them rushing to the scene of the encounter, Ella sat alone, and for now, that was good. She replayed the encounter with the smaller worm, the one presumed female, her scientific side processing the events. First, it attacked her for reasons unknown. Then it was close enough to strike but didn't for reasons unknown. The encounter haunted her and would, she expected, for a long time. She wanted to understand. She *needed* to know why it spared her. Why her and not Rodion? Or the camel? Who was she to be left alive?

She remained there, still and silent, as people came and went, many wandering close enough to confirm she was fine then hurry off. She hardly noticed as the first hint of the new day dawned on the horizon. This was it, day ten. Time to go home.

Finally, one of the teens came and silently offered her a plate of bread and cheese, but none of the disgusting salted milk foods. Someone had finally paid attention. She nibbled at the day-old bread, drinking more water, but it was tasteless. She chewed slowly, lost in her thoughts.

In time, the camp sounds settled into routine ones. Cooking and eating and talking. Laughter even rose amidst the carnage and loss. It sounded wrong to her.

Lebedev sat beside her, holding a cup of milk tea, sipping at it slowly.

"How are you?"

"Numb," she admitted.

"That may be for the best," he said. He sipped and considered what to say next. "We've secured the dead Death Worm. It's packed and ready for transport. There were eleven eggs, which we managed to weigh and measure before packing those away. With such evidence, we can finally confirm the legend, but more importantly, we have new things to study and learn."

"What about Rodion? And Vlaerik?"

There was a long pause before he spoke. "Well, yes, I mean, they sacrificed themselves for the mission, but both knew the expedition was not without danger. Rodion always understood that, and I think the poor boy came to realize we were serious."

"I meant, what about their bodies?"

That stopped the older man. He swallowed a word, then sipped to buy a moment. "Well, they've been wrapped up. They will be transported with us and then flown home. No doubt there will be an inquest, possibly an autopsy, before the bodies are released for international travel."

"Oh."

They sat in more silence, and then Ella asked, "The Mongolian authorities are going to just let you leave with the greatest scientific find in, I don't know, centuries?"

"We have our clearances from the Kremlin. We can let the authorities look in the interests of international cooperation, but then we have already received permission to bring the specimens obtained on the expedition back to Russia."

"Why?"

"Why what?"

"Why would Mongolia relinquish control of something of such import?" she asked. Her mind had been working through the matter ever since she arrived. It felt wrong. Like when cultural artifacts were taken as souvenirs by conquering armies, dating back through history.

"I can't speak to the politics of the matter, but the Kremlin usually gets what it wants."

"And why does the Kremlin want a Mongolian Death Worm?"

Lebedev looked at her, his eyes going from grandfatherly to something else, something darker. He clearly was composing a response in his head, debating how much to say. She just wanted an answer, one she could believe, preferably the truth.

"Doctor, I signed every waiver and legal document you waved under my nose. I can be a good girl and say nothing, and by now, I think I can be trusted."

"I suppose you can," he said after a long moment. "And I suppose you deserve some sort of answer after all this. After losing your... friend."

"He was something more than that, you know."

"How much more?"

"I'll never know for sure," she admitted.

"Well, apparently, someone in the Kremlin came across an old file, one about the specimen Rodion showed you. They were intrigued by the acid. The world is always looking for new ways to kill, and this seemed a fresh avenue."

"They wanted to *weaponize* the Death Worm?" This appalled her on many levels. As a human, she was horrified. As a scientist, insulted. As an American, outraged... and torn as to what she should do. Legally, she signed non-disclosure agreements. But patriotically, it was her duty to report this. Of course, she could imagine the government's reaction should she try and report this. Who would believe her? And where could she turn? CIA? State Department? Department of Defense? Internally, turmoil thrashed near as much as the slain worm had.

"No, they wanted the acid, how to make it, how to use it. It was worth a few hundred thousand rubles to find out if the legends were true and if so, what could be learned."

"Rather than some scientific trip to find some new species, we were hunting for the next WMD?"

"WMD? I don't follow; maybe it's the translation," Lebedev said.

"Weapon of mass destruction," she said flatly.

His eyes narrowed as the words seeped in, and then nodded in understanding.

"Isn't this some sort of betrayal of principal?" Ella challenged.

"Maybe, but that's not for me to say. I don't like to debate these matters. That's for others to discuss. I am a scientist."

"You're also complicit..." She left the words 'in murder' unsaid, falling silent. His gaze hardened, but he said nothing, merely turning and returning to their ger. Still, unease roiled in her belly. A lot could happen in the desert. She depended on the expedition to get her home, particularly now, with Rodion gone.

Deep within her, however, she wanted to scream her accusations from the mountaintops.

Back in their ger, it was clear none of the others were going to pack up Rodion's belongings to be returned to his family. She used the time to savor his scent, recall moments when he wore a particular shirt or item. It was methodical work, and it gave her time to think. If the government really wanted the cryptid for a weapon, then it perverted the goal of science and research. It made her feel foolish for even contemplating staying in a country ruled by people who would condone such things. Not that America was necessarily any better. She would like to think they were above this sort of thing, though a part of her knew better. But, in America, she didn't have to do work for government-funded projects. there were plenty of commercial and non-profit options available. As she packed the last of his things, securing the baggage, she wondered would there have been a way to convince him to follow *her*? Would his Russian ego have allowed for that? Had he loved her enough?

Someone cleared their throat, catching her attention. Lebedev gestured for her to join him outside the ger. She followed, curious, but mostly tired. The scientist did not look happy, which worried her anew.

"I have spoken with the university," he said then hesitated.

"What's wrong?"

"They have heard from me and Sgt. Yegorov and taken all of three hours to render a decision, which for them is fast." He let out a rumbling short laugh. This was not funny to her.

"I have been instructed to inform you that your internship in Russia has been extended indefinitely. You will accompany us to

Moscow. First, you will be debriefed." His voice had dropped, it was a serious tone, and it sounded more recitation than heartfelt.

"I don't understand. How long is indefinitely? Why?" She felt something drop in her stomach, a chill running down her arms despite the desert heat.

"Everything you did was valuable, and I told them that. They want you to consider this a kind of reward."

She shook her head in disbelief.

"I am expected back in the states. My graduate program... my parents... they're expecting me in weeks. Are you worried I am going to say something? It's not like I want to relive any of this — besides, who is going to believe me? Unless you publicly disclose the existence of the Mongolian Death Worm, no one will accept that. And you're not going to go public with your latest weapon, are you?"

He brooded at that, but his silence was the answer.

"What about Chenghiz or Jargal or the kids?"

"Arrangements are being made to buy their silence. They are merely nomads with yet another tall tale to tell."

"But my cell phone has video proof. Won't that confirm their tales?"

Lebedev shook his head slowly. "We could not find it."

But he would not meet her eyes. He left unsaid the truth that she would never see that phone again, losing her contact with home.

"If I bring the American consulate into this, this won't end well, will it? I'll be questioned at home, maybe hounded. I'd really rather not think about this again."

"You won't have a chance to speak to the consulate. We are asking you stay on to help us investigate the worm," he said sounding once more like the grandfather. "This will also weigh heavily on me."

She let out a scoffing sound. "I am a mammalian specialist," she protested. "And I never want to see that thing again."

"After your meeting, you will be checked by our doctors, and then begin your new assignment.

"For you or for the KGB?"

He chuckled. "They no longer exist. The new letters are SVR."

"Whatever. In other words, I am now a prisoner of Russia."

Lebedev didn't react to the statement, but his lack of protest confirmed her growing fears.

Dazed and angry, she limped away from the scientist, who just sat there and let her go. Ella entered the ger. Neither Kozlov nor Smirnov would meet her eyes. She turned her attention to her own things, similarly recalling a shirt Rodion once worked his way inside or a bracelet he liked. Her mind replayed the previous hours, the confrontation with the Death Worm and its uncharacteristic — or was it — behavior at the end? She was certainly fascinated by the way it dug deep so quickly. She'd never seen anything like that in her studies. But she froze the image of the Death Worm, close enough to smell its alien odor, well within striking distance. It had looked hesitant, evaluating maybe? Why? Was it because Ella was a female? Was there some other external factor that caused to it pause, then flee?

Then a though… a possibility struck her.

She left the packing incomplete and went to find Grisha. He was in the process of securing their gear, awaiting the trucks' arrival, when he spotted her and gave a tentative wave.

"How are you?" she asked in Russian, her words only slightly halting.

"Fine, fine… But what about you?" he said.

"I don't think I'll be fine until I am home," she admitted. "Did you know Vlaerik well?"

"Well enough, I suppose. We hadn't served together before being assigned to this trip. He had just come off a rotation and was awaiting reassignment and well, this happened."

"He seemed nice enough," she said.

"A good soldier."

Nodding, Ella glanced around them. Seeing no one else in the area, she switched to English her words still halting, if for other reasons.

"Grisha… you know that Rodion and I… well, we… we were together, yes?"

His expression a touch curious, the medic nodded.

Flushing, Ella murmured, "I need the test from your medical supplies."

His eyes went wide, his gaze dropping to her abdomen, but he nodded again, without comment or judgment. "Da," he answered. "Wait here."

Ella nodded, though he'd already turned and headed for his own ger. She trembled, feeling a bit queasy, as she looked out across the desert seeing possible worm sign in every ripple in the sand. At a gentle touch on her arm, Ella jumped, almost losing her footing as the sand shifted beneath her feet. Grisha caught her in a firm grip and steadied her before holding out the kit she'd requested.

As she accepted it, she caught Grisha's hand and held his gaze, her expression fierce.

"No one. You must tell *no one*."

Silently, he nodded.

Fifteen minutes later, Ella's hand went to her abdomen, an uneasy cocktail of awe and panic and wonder churning in her gut. Was this why she'd survived her encounter with the Death Worm? Had it… had *she* instinctively withdrawn, rather than kill another expectant mother?

Ella liked to believe so.

Back in the ger, she was left to herself. Her body felt alien to her, another force derailing her plans. In the last few hours, she seemed to have lost her lover, her cell phone, and her freedom. In exchange, Ella carried a child she now wanted to protect, and was being assigned to study something no one else had ever examined. She would be making history and no one would ever know. She would never see her parents or friends again, never travel the world to study as she had dreamed. Were the tradeoffs balanced out?

An engine started nearby, the truck readying to take everyone back to the airport and then back to Russia. There, she'd embark on something new and had the entire ride to contemplate what it all meant, and what her baby's future held.

For now, though, the worm carcass and the unfertilized eggs awaited her. She and her own growing embryo rose and limped from the ger. The desert gave up one secret only to swallow her life in the process.

ABOUT THE AUTHOR

Robert Greenberger is a writer and editor. A lifelong fan of comic books, comic strips, science fiction, and *Star Trek*, he drifted towards writing and editing, encouraged by his father and inspired by Superman's alter ego, Clark Kent.

While at SUNY-Binghamton, Greenberger wrote and edited for the college newspaper, *Pipe Dream*. Upon graduation, he worked for Starlog Press and while there, created *Comics Scene*, the first nationally distributed magazine to focus on comic books, comic strips, and animation.

In 1984, he joined DC Comics as an Assistant Editor and went on to be an Editor before moving to Administration as Manager-Editorial Operations. He joined Gist Communications as a Producer before moving to Marvel Comics as its Director-Publishing Operations.

Greenberger rejoined DC in May 2002 as a Senior Editor-Collected Editions. He helped grow that department, introducing new formats and improving the editions' editorial content. In 2006, he joined *Weekly World News* as its Managing Editor until the paper's untimely demise. He then freelanced for an extensive client base including Platinum Studios, scifi.com, DC, and Marvel. He helped revitalize *Famous Monsters of Filmland* and served as News Editor at ComicMix.com.

He is a member of the Science Fiction Writers of America and the International Association of Media Tie-In Writers. His novelization of *Hellboy II: The Golden Army* won the IAMTW's Scribe Award in 2009.

In 2012, he received his Master of Science in Education from the University of Bridgeport and relocated to Maryland where he has taught High School English in Baltimore County. He completed his Master of Arts degree in Creative Writing & Literature for Educators at Fairleigh Dickinson University in 2016.

With others, he co-founded Crazy 8 Press, a digital press hub where he continues to write. His dozens of books, short stories, and essays cover the gamut from young adult nonfiction to original fiction. His most recent works include Chartwell Books' *100 Greatest Moments* series, *The Dreadstar Handbook*, and editing *Thrilling Adventure Yarns*.

Bob teaches High School English at St. Vincent Pallotti High School in Laurel, MD. He and his wife Deborah reside in Howard County, Maryland. Find him at www.bobgreenberger.com or @bobgreenberger.

ABOUT THE ARTIST

Although Jason Whitley has worn many creative hats, he is at heart a traditional illustrator and painter. With author James Chambers, Jason collaborates and illustrates the sometimes-prose, sometimes graphic novel, *The Midnight Hour,* which is being collected into one volume by eSpec Books. His and Scott Eckelaert's newspaper comic strip, Sea Urchins, has been collected into four volumes. Along with eSpec Books' Systema Paradoxa series, Jason is working on a crime noir graphic novel. His portrait of Charlotte Hawkins Brown is on display in the Charlotte Hawkins Brown Museum.

artist's rendition of the Mongolian Death Worm

MONGOLIAN DEATH WORM

(Also known as
Olgoi-Khorkhoi)

ORIGIN: Long known among the nomadic tribes of the Gobi Desert as the large intestine worm in their native tongue, this cryptid hails specifically from that region. Though the desert encompasses 500,000 miles, this burrowing Worm is reported to inhabit the western or southern regions, where the desert is the most desolate.

DESCRIPTION: While there is some debate if this creature is, in fact, a worm, it is described as the shape of a sausage, with either a pink, blood red, or dark crimson color skin, no visible eyes or ears, and spikes protruding from either end of its body. Specimens are said to range between two and seven feet long. As worms absorb oxygen through their skin, it is possible for them to grow to the immense size reported for the Death Worm.

Among its natural defenses are the ability to spit an acidic poison or strike out with an electric discharge, both capable of killing an adult human instantly. The Worm itself is said to be poisonous to the touch and its acid is corrosive, leaving everything it touches a corroded yellow color. These creatures travel underground, leaving no more than a tell-tale wave pattern in the sand above, but are said to surface more often during the rainy period, in June and July.

Some theorize that the Mongolian Death Worm is not a worm, which would not be expected to survive the harsh environs of the desert, but perhaps a new species of worm-lizard, reptiles also known for burrowing. However, there is precedence for sand-dwelling worms, such at the Australian beach worm to lend credence to a desert-dwelling species.

Others believe sightings are the result of hallucinations or misidentification of various species of snakes of similar description, such as the pit viper, rat snake, or sand boa. Some have even suggested these are accounts of a type of skink, though that theory is discounted as skinks have legs and scaled skin. All speculation is based on second- and third-hand accounts.

LIFE CYCLE: Unknown.

HISTORY: Due to Soviet control of the region until 1990, there is little knowledge of the Death Worm in the west. Since then, there have been many expeditions in search of this creature or evidence of its existence, but to date, none of them have been successful. However, there are those in the field of cryptozoology who have not ruled out the existence of the Mongolian Death Worm, due to the vastness of its habitat, as well as the number of reported sightings and strange deaths. Many believe this cryptid to be more than just legend, though more concrete evidence is needed to satisfy the scientific community.

Capture the Cryptids!

Cryptid Crate is a monthly subscription box filled with various cryptozoology and paranormal-themed items to wear, display, and collect. Expect a carefully curated box filled with creeptastic pieces from indie makers and artisans pertaining to bigfoot, sasquatch, UFOs, ghosts, and other cryptid and mysterious creatures (apparel, decor, media, etc).

Now Featuring Cryptid Crate Jr.!

http://CryptidCrate.com

Printed in the USA
CPSIA information can be obtained
at www.ICGtesting.com
JSHW081958170923
48387JS00003B/9